A MATTER OF CLASS

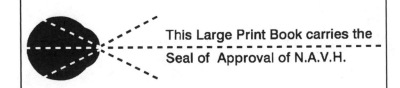

This Large Print Book carries the
Seal of Approval of N.A.V.H.

A MATTER OF CLASS

MARY BALOGH

THORNDIKE PRESS

A part of Gale, Cengage Learning

GALE
CENGAGE Learning·

Detroit • New York • San Francisco • New Haven, Conn • Waterville, Maine • London

GALE
CENGAGE Learning™

Copyright © 2010 by Mary Balogh.
Thorndike Press, a part of Gale, Cengage Learning.

ALL RIGHTS RESERVED
Thorndike Press® Large Print Core.
The text of this Large Print edition is unabridged.
Other aspects of the book may vary from the original edition.
Set in 16 pt. Plantin.
Printed on permanent paper.

LIBRARY OF CONGRESS CATALOGING-IN-PUBLICATION DATA

Balogh, Mary.
 A matter of class / by Mary Balogh.
  p. cm. — (Thorndike Press large print core)
 ISBN-13: 978-1-4104-2341-2 (alk. paper)
 ISBN-10: 1-4104-2341-7 (alk. paper)
 1. Large type books. I. Title.
PR6052.A465M38 2009b
823'.914—dc22   2009040633

Published in 2009 by arrangement with Maria Carvainis Agency.

Printed in the United States of America
1 2 3 4 5 6 7 14 13 12 11 10

To Maria Carvainis, my agent,
and to June Renschler,
Jerome Murphy,
and Alex Slater, her assistants,
who are all and always
in my corner.

1

Reginald Mason crossed one elegantly clad leg over the other and contemplated the gold tassel swinging from one of his white-topped Hessian boots. The boots had been just one of many recent extravagances, but what was one to do when fashions shifted almost daily and one had been taught from the cradle onward that keeping up appearances was of the utmost importance?

What one *could* do, of course, was ignore the almost daily vagaries of fashion and instead aim for basic good grooming, and that was what he had always done — until the past year, when, for reasons of his own, he had chosen to pursue the path of high fashion.

It was his father who had drummed the lesson of keeping up appearances into him. Bernard Mason was not a gentleman by birth but rather a self-made man who had spent lavishly of his enormous wealth on all the trappings of gentility, including the very best education for his only son and a large country estate in Wiltshire. He was, by his own estimation, lord of all he surveyed — except the world of the beau monde, which looked down upon him along its collective nose as a very inferior being and an upstart to boot. As a consequence, he heartily despised the *ton* — and dreamed incessantly of finding a way into its hallowed ranks. His son was his greatest hope for accomplishing that dream.

All of these facts made it illogical that he was so furiously angry now, that he had been angry all too often during the past several months. For Reggie had been behaving exactly as a young gentleman of *ton* was expected to behave in order to demonstrate his superiority over the mass of ordinary mortals who must perforce be more intent upon earning money than spending it. He had been as extravagant and reckless and idle as the best of his would-be peers.

His father was sitting a short distance from Reggie, though the wide expanse of the solid oak desk in his study stood between them and set them symbolically much farther apart. The wildly successful and prudent businessman confronted his wildly expensive, aimless, and profligate son with thunderous displeasure. He had just finished delivering an eloquent lecture on the theme of worthless cubs — not for the first time. Reggie had been told, loudly enough to imply that he must be deaf as well as daft, that a man who aspired to be accepted as a gentleman must give all the appearance of gentility, good breeding, and wealth without dabbling in any of its attendant vices.

And Reginald had done more than dabble.

Was it a vice to buy the very best and most fashionable of boots? Reggie jiggled his foot slightly and watched the tassel sway into motion again. It glinted in the sunlight beaming through the window.

He sat half-slouched in his hard wooden chair as a visual sign of his apparent unconcern. He did consider yawning, but that would be going too far.

"Anyone would think, lad," his father said after a few moments of exasperated silence, "that you were out to beggar me."

His use of the word *lad* was not, in this instance, an endearment. It was his father's way of speaking. Whereas Reggie's expensive education had polished his speech until it was indistinguishable from that of the beau monde, his father still spoke with a broad and unabashed North country accent.

It would take far more than his recent extravagances to beggar his father, Reggie knew. A little excessive and expensive attention to his wardrobe and a little unlucky gambling would put scarcely a dent in his father's fortune, nor even a fair amount of unlucky gambling, which was probably a more accurate and only slightly understated description of his recent losses.

Reggie swallowed the uneasy sense of guilt that rose into his throat like bile.

"That there curricle, now," his father began, stabbing the desk top with the tip of one broad finger, as though the offending vehicle were cowering beneath it.

Reggie cut him off. He risked a bored cadence to his voice.

"Any self-respecting gentleman below the age of thirty-five," he said, "must have a racing curricle as well as one for simply tooling about town, sir. And you *do* wish me to be a gentleman, do you not?"

His father's face took on a slightly purple hue.

"And a matched pair of grays to go with it?" he said, still poking at the desk. "The chestnuts you purchased *last month* would not do the job?"

Reggie shuddered elegantly.

"They do not match the paint-work," he said, his voice pained. "Besides, they are all prancing show, perfect for impressing the ladies in Hyde Park, but quite useless if I should decide to race the new curricle to Brighton. You *would* wish me to win, would you not?"

"And serve you right if you were to break your neck in the attempt," his father said brusquely. "I am going to have to lease more stable room."

Reggie simply shrugged.

"And these . . . *debts*," his father said, picking up a sheaf of papers from one side of the desk in his large fist and waving them in the direction of his son's nose. "You expect me to pay them, I suppose?"

They *were* large. Most of them were gaming debts. Reggie never left the card tables or the races until he had lost. Whenever he surprised himself by winning, he always stayed until he had lost all the money again and sent plenty more in chase of it.

"If you please, sir," he said with a weary sigh.

His father's bushy eyebrows collided above his nose.

"If I please?" he barked wrathfully, and he squeezed the bills in his hand and dropped them onto the desk. They fanned out into an alarmingly large heap. "Was it for this that I brought you into the world, Reginald, and spent a king's ransom to have you educated as a gentleman? Was it not rather that I might see and enjoy the fruits of my labors in my old age? I will never be accepted by all the high and mighty *gentlemen* of this realm. I will always reek of coal in their pampered, perfumed noses. And that is just grand as far as I am concerned. I have no interest in rubbing shoulders with popinjays. I despise the lot of them. But *you* . . . you could have the best of it all. You could be my son *and* a gentleman."

15

Reggie shrugged and refrained from pointing out the lack of logic in his father's attitude toward the beau monde.

"I am accepted well enough by all the gentlemen I know," he said. "I went to school with half of them. As for the ladies, well, who needs them? There are plenty of *women* who are far more, ah, interesting." He made a careless, dismissive gesture with one well-manicured hand.

His father's large hand slammed down flat on the desk.

"If you were to settle down with a good woman, lad," he said, "you would be less trouble to me and more of a gentleman to boot."

"Time enough to think of that," Reggie said hastily, "when I am thirty-five or so. I have at least ten

years of good living to do before set-
tling down."

He would have been better advised
to keep his mouth shut. His father's
eyes narrowed in a familiar look. His
mind had latched onto a subject and
was giving it shrewd consideration.
And that subject — Reggie knew it
even before his father spoke again —
was matrimony. Specifically as it
concerned his son.

"You will marry into gentility, Reginald," he said. "Even into nobility.
You are handsome enough, God
knows, having had the good fortune
to take after your mother's side of
the family instead of mine. And you
are rich enough — or will be if I do
not cut you off without a penny."

As well as standing to inherit the
whole of his father's vast fortune,

Reggie was the sort-of owner of Willows End, a sizable home and estate in Hampshire, a sort-of gift on his twenty-first birthday four years ago. Exclusive ownership was to pass to him on his thirtieth birthday or on his wedding day, whichever came first. Or the gift could simply be withdrawn if he was deemed unworthy of it before either of those dates hove into sight. The threat had never been made — until now.

"No one in the upper echelons will have me," Reggie pointed out, rubbing one finger over what might have been a small smudge on the inside of his boot. "Not for a husband."

"*Someone* will," his father said viciously. "All we have to do is keep our eyes and ears open and wait for the right opportunity."

"But not for the next ten years or so," Reggie said firmly. "There is no hurry. I am perfectly happy as I am for now."

It was the wrong thing to say again. His father impaled him with a ferocious glare.

"But I am *not*," he said. "I am not at all happy, Reginald. I do not know what has happened to you of late. I used to think myself the most fortunate of fathers. I used to think you the very best of sons," he sighed. "I shall start looking for a bride for you without any further delay. And I shall look high. I will not waste you on some obscure gentleman's daughter."

"No!" Reginald said firmly, uncrossing his legs and straightening out of his slouch. "I will not marry simply to please you, sir. Not even if you were able to persuade one of the royal princesses to have me."

His father's heavy eyebrows soared halfway up his forehead.

"To *please* me?" he said. "You do not please me at all, Reginald. You have not pleased me — *or your mother* — for some time now. She pleads your case by telling me that you are merely sowing your wild oats. If that is so, you have sown far too many of them for long enough. You will marry, lad, as soon as I have found you a suitable bride, and you will settle down and live a respectable life."

"I beg your pardon," Reggie said, a thread of steel in his voice now even though he spoke politely enough, "but you cannot force me, sir."

"You are right," his father said, his voice dipping ominously in volume.

"I cannot. But I *can* cut off your funds, Reginald, and that would be like cutting off the air you breathe. I can and I will do it if you refuse to offer marriage to the first lady I find for you."

Reggie leaned back in his chair and stared at his father's angry, implacable face. The threat was explicit now.

"You ought to be thankful," he said, "that I have never done anything actually to disgrace you, sir, as some members of the *nobility* have done to *their* fathers. Ladies as well as gentlemen. You have heard about Lady Annabelle Ashton, I suppose?"

Lady Annabelle was the daughter of the Earl of Havercroft, whose country estate adjoined the Mason property in Wiltshire. And if there was one member of the *ton* whom Reggie's father hated more than any other, it was Havercroft. Bernard Mason had bought his property thirty years ago when his fortune had been made and had moved there with high hopes of moving also into a different world. He had extended the hand of friendship to his neighbor only to find that hand left dangling in the cold, empty air. The earl had chosen not only to snub him for his presumption, but also to ignore his very existence. He had instructed his family and all who were dependent upon him to do likewise. Mason, not to be outdone, had first denounced Havercroft as a conceited fop and then ordered *his* family and servants never so much as to *look* in his direction or that of his wife and daughter.

The best families in the neighborhood trod the tightrope of maintaining civil relations with both of their powerful neighbors without alienating either. But their loyalties leaned toward the earl. They paid him open homage whenever he was in residence — which was mercifully infrequently — and were quietly polite to the Masons without actually including them in their social life. They would mingle with him at local assemblies only because the earl never attended them.

It had not been a comfortable thirty years. Reggie had grown up in that atmosphere of mutual hatred and scorn. He had actually come to derive some amusement from Sunday mornings at church whenever both families were in residence. Masons and Ashcrofts occupied front pews on either side of the aisle and acted as if the other family did not exist — except that, for the two men, the whole thing was ostentatious, the earl haughtily contemptuous of the family that did not exist, and Reggie's father loudly hearty as he greeted everyone except the family that did not exist. And his north country accent was always broader than usual on Sunday mornings.

"Eh?" his father said now. "What about her?"

Reggie snickered.

"She ran off with Havercroft's new coachman a few nights ago," he said. "A handsome devil, by all accounts. They did not get more than a dozen miles on their way to the Scottish border, though, before being caught and hauled back to town. At least, *she* was hauled back. The coachman, coward as he was, made his escape from a window at the inn where they were apprehended, and since his mashed remains were not discovered under it, it was assumed that he made his escape. Unfortunately, the two of them were seen by half the world before they were overtaken, and by now most of the *other* half of the world knows all about it too — with embellishments, I do not doubt. She is disgraced. Ruined. Illingsworth has withdrawn his suit, as one might expect, and no other man is stepping up to take his place. She will be fortunate if she can find a chimney sweep to marry her."

He flicked a spot of lint off the sleeve of his coat.

His father was staring at him, slack-jawed.

"*Illingsworth* has withdrawn?" he said. "He is as rich as Croesus, or rather his father the duke is, anyway. How is Havercroft going to manage now?"

It was widely known that the Earl of Havercroft had made some rash investments a few years ago and that, in anticipation of making a huge profit from them, he had undertaken extensive and exorbitantly expensive renovations to his country home last year. And then his investments had collapsed. All Season he had been single-mindedly courting Illingsworth for his daughter, his one remaining asset if he was to escape from dire financial straits.

"Ruined, is she?" Reggie's father

said softly, and he smiled unseeingly into the middle distance.

Reggie became suddenly alert. His hand stilled over his sleeve.

"I am *not*," he said, standing up abruptly and setting both hands flat on the desk, "going to marry a woman who ran off with a *servant*, for the love of God. Even if she is a lady. *With a title.* And even if you *are* visualizing marvelous revenge on your mortal enemy. If that is what you *are* contemplating, sir, you may forget it without further ado. I will not do it. Your quarrel with Havercroft is not mine."

His father slapped one hand on the desk.

"*Ruined* is she?" he said again just as if he had not even heard his son's alarmed protest.

Reggie watched in tense silence as his father's mind worked over these salacious new facts concerning his neighbor — facts that suddenly gave him the power he had always craved. He was still smiling. It was not a pleasant sight.

"Ruined, is she?" he said once more, and he got to his feet and faced his son almost nose to nose across the desk. He was broad of frame and thick of waist — in contrast to Reggie's slim elegance. But they were of a height with each other. "Ee, lad, *now* we will see a thing or two. *Now* we will see who is high and mighty and who is decent enough to condescend to save him. *Now* we will see if a neighbor's hand of sympathy and friendship is not shaken after all."

Reggie spoke through lips stiff with

apprehension. He could feel a prickle of perspiration trickling down his back beneath his shirt. He could actually *hear* his heartbeat.

"You are going to call upon Havercroft to offer neighborly sympathy?" he said. "Nothing else?"

His father shook his head in exasperation at his son's obtuseness.

"For a man who was so expensively educated, Reginald," he said, "you can be awfully daft. *Of course* I am going to offer sympathy and the hand of friendship. What are neighbors for if they can't stick together in times of trouble? But I'll offer sympathy not just in the form of airy words, lad. Anyone can offer those. My sympathy will be more practical, as has always been my way. I am going to show him a road out of his financial troubles and a way to lift his daughter out of ruin at the same time. A coal merchant's son will be more desirable than a chimney sweep, I don't doubt. I am going to offer him *you*."

He glared in triumph at his son.

"And if you don't like it, lad," he added, "you have only yourself to blame. You are my flesh and blood and I have always doted on you, but right now I would have to say you deserve a haughty, *ruined* little chit for your own. And she deserves you."

Reggie sank heavily back into his seat.

He had a strong conviction that nothing he might say would persuade his father to change his mind. He must try anyway. His father was clearly expecting it of him. He had resumed his seat behind the desk and was rubbing his hands together in anticipatory glee.

Reggie swallowed, only to find that there was not one drop of saliva in his mouth.

There was no telling yet how Havercroft would react to the proposition his father was clearly determined to make, but this match was already halfway made.

If the other half did not fall into place, he might find himself permanently estranged from his father. And Lady Annabelle Ashton might — no, *would* — find herself ruined beyond repair.

Reggie licked his lips with a dry tongue and prepared to argue. For the moment, it was all he could do.

Lady Annabelle Ashton, who was

renowned for the rose-petal complexion that complemented her very blond hair so becomingly, was now of a complexion that *matched* her hair. She was as pale as a ghost.

It did not matter that Thomas Till had been the perfect gentleman throughout their escapade, that she had not been alone with him for very long at all, and that for most of that time she had been inside the carriage, and he up on the box driving it. It did not matter that he had never touched more than her hand as he helped her in and out of the carriage and then into the inn where they had been imprudent enough to stop for refreshments as well as a change of horses. It did not matter that he was gone from her life now, never to be a part of it again — or that she did not even know where he was. It did not matter that from the moment she had been apprehended, she had guarded the state of her heart with silent, stubborn dignity.

None of it mattered as far as society was concerned. She was ruined anyway.

For she and Thomas had committed an unpardonable indiscretion. They had been seen leaving the Bomford ball together — at least, *she* had been seen leaving in the middle of the ball with no chaperon except her father's handsome new coachman. And they had been seen by half the inhabitants of Berkeley Square and half the servants at Havercroft House there when they had stopped for her to pick up her portmanteau from her bedchamber. Thomas had actually carried it downstairs for her and out the front doors. They had been seen by all the ostlers and grooms and indoor servants and a large number of travelers and other customers at the busy, fashionable inn where they had chosen to stop on their journey north.

And, of course, though Thomas had only touched her hand at the inn while leading her to a table for refreshments, one of those touches had been with his lips in an extravagantly courtly gesture for all to see.

Wearing his coachman's livery, no less.

Annabelle was disgraced. Ruined. For all time. Forever and ever, amen. There was no hope for her, short of a miracle. Her confidence, which she had always possessed in no small measure, had been shaken to the core.

She would dwindle into a shriveled old maid — though *spinster* was the word her father had used, avoiding the whole concept of maidenhood. She would spend the rest of her life in sequestered obscurity, unwanted and unlamented.

Untouchable.

No man would ever have her now.

Just last week, half the gentlemen of the *ton* would gladly have had her — the ones who were single, anyway. She was reputed to be a rare beauty.

That was what she had been. Past tense.

Now the whole of the male world of *ton* would turn their backs on her if she should be foolish enough to appear before them. The *female* world would do worse. They would sweep from the room, their skirts held close to their persons lest they brush inadvertently against air that had also brushed against her, their noses all but scraping the ceiling as they went.

She was a pariah.

And she had brought it all on herself. She had stepped quite deliberately over the brink, confident that her life would unfold as she had planned it to unfold.

Now she could only feel a wave of panic clutching her stomach. She could no longer direct the course of her life. For the present at least she was totally at the mercy of outside forces, most notably her father.

It was the most wretched feeling she could possibly imagine.

She was not going to be sent back

to Oakridge Park, the country home in Wiltshire where she had been brought up, her father's principal seat. Even there she might contaminate the neighbors, who so respected her father. Instead she was to be sent into the outer darkness of Meadow Hall close to the Scottish border, a minor property of her father's, which did not in any way live up to its name. Or so she had heard. She had never been there to see for herself. But that was about to change. It was where she was destined to spend the rest of her mortal days.

Barring a miracle.

She no longer believed in plans, no matter how carefully made. She was afraid to believe. She had been a fool.

Her mother was not going to be allowed to go with her, even though she had wept and pleaded and cajoled and even lost her temper — a rare occurrence that had filled Annabelle with a terrible guilt. Mama ought not to be made to suffer. But of course she *was* suffering.

At this precise moment, Annabelle was still in London, where she had been enjoying the entertainments of the Season before dashing off with Thomas Till. Though *enjoying* was not quite the right word. How could she enjoy herself when the man she loved could not similarly enjoy the same events and she could see him only rarely and under very clandestine circumstances? And how could she enjoy herself when she had been given strict orders to encourage the attentions of a man she loathed simply because he was rich enough to pay off Papa's debts in exchange for her hand in marriage?

Her father had been diligently courting the Marquess of Illingsworth for her all Season and had been confident of success. The marquess was only fourteen years older than she and only half a head shorter and only half bald. *And* he was besotted with her. She had nothing whatsoever to complain of — at least that's what Papa had always said whenever she *had* complained.

She was shut up in her room, from which all books — except the Bible — and embroidery and painting and writing supplies had been ostentatiously removed lest she find some way of amusing herself and forgetting her plight. And the door had been locked from the outside so that she could be in no doubt that she was a prisoner at her father's pleasure.

She felt like the worst sort of criminal.

Two days of incarceration had felt like two weeks or two months. Each hour had seemed a day long. Perhaps, Annabelle thought all too frequently, she had made the biggest mistake of her life when she fled with Thomas.

And sometimes she thought there was no *perhaps* about it.

The window of her bedchamber overlooked a small kitchen garden and a maze of stables and coach houses behind it. There was very little to look out upon and no way at all of knowing who — if anyone — rode into the square at the front of the house and maybe even stopped outside their door.

Perhaps no one did.

Perhaps no one ever would.

The bottom threatened to fall out of her stomach. Oh, how she *hated* this helplessness. She had never been helpless. Quite the contrary.

And then she heard the distant sound of the door knocker banging against the front door.

It might be anyone, of course.

Indeed, it almost undoubtedly was *someone.*

Annabelle shocked herself by giggling aloud at the sad joke. She clapped one hand over her mouth.

It was best not to hope. But how could one *not* hope? What else was there to live for?

More than half an hour went by before the key scraped in the lock of her door and the door swung inward to reveal her father on the threshold, frowning sternly as usual, and her mother behind his right shoulder, smiling encouragement at her, tears in her eyes, her face pale and wan.

Annabelle stood and clasped her hands at her waist.

She felt slightly sick to the stomach. Guilt was a horrible feeling, and she was staring it in the face when she glanced at her mother. Apprehension was just as bad. What now? Was the carriage ready at the door to bear her off into outer darkness?

"Well, miss," her father said, stepping inside the room and seeming to half fill it with his tall, imposing figure. When he frowned, his great hooked nose made him look even more like a bird of prey than usual. "You are to have better than you deserve."

Her mother nodded and dabbed at a spilled-over tear with one index finger.

Annabelle said nothing.

"I have been persuaded to lower my standards in order to restore at least a modicum of respectability to my family," he said, "though it will be a long time before I will forgive you for forcing it upon me, Annabelle. My only consolation is that you will suffer more than your mother and I, and that you will deserve exactly what you get."

His lips stretched into a grimace that might have been intended as a smile. Not a smile of pleasure or amusement or affection, however.

Gracious heaven, Annabelle thought, darting a glance at her

mother, who was swiping at another tear, whatever did he *mean?* The Marquess of Illingsworth had not offered for her after all, had he? Had Papa never been close enough to him to smell his *breath?* Or to see his *teeth?* Had her bold bid for freedom really failed so utterly and so miserably?

But Papa had *lowered his standards?*

"I have just had a visit from Mason," he said, clasping his hands at his back.

Annabelle's eyes widened. There was a sudden coldness in her head that threatened a fainting fit. It took a conscious physical effort to draw a breath into her lungs.

"Mr. *Mason?*" she asked foolishly as though her father had spoken too quietly to be heard clearly.

Mr. Mason was their neighbor at Oakridge. He was enormously wealthy and enormously . . . well, large. He was also, if her father was to be believed, enormously vulgar, uncouth, and any number of other unsavory, low things. In other words, he was not one of *them*. He was not a gentleman. He had made his fortune in coal and still had coal dust encrusted beneath his fingernails — according to Papa. And he had had the unmitigated gall to purchase the estate adjoining Papa's when it was for sale many years ago. He had pulled down the old house and built an expensively vulgar mansion in its place and had set out to be *amiable,* to be accepted as an equal by no less a person than the Earl of Havercroft.

He was an upstart — a dreadful thing to be if one's family happened to have been of the nobility for countless generations back. Probably as far back as the Conquest.

Mr. Mason had been Papa's mortal enemy for as long as Annabelle could recall. She and Mama had not been allowed to acknowledge him or Mrs. Mason even when they were occasionally at church together. They had not been allowed even so much as to *look* at the Masons or to recognize that they existed. It would puff them up to unbearable proportions, Papa had always said, and encourage further impudence.

Now Mr. Mason had come *calling?*

"Did you admit him, Papa?" Annabelle asked.

"I had him shown into Palmer's office, not the visitors' parlor," he said. "But he would not state his business to anyone but me."

Mr. Palmer was Papa's secretary.

"I was obliged to see him," her father said.

Yes, of course he was. Mr. Mason was *rich.* And Papa was really quite frighteningly poor after losing all that money recently and spending so lavishly last summer.

"He came to offer you marriage," her father added.

"Mr. *Mason* did?" she asked, her voice a distressed squeak.

"Oh, Annabelle," her mother said, speaking for the first time. "*Mrs.* Mason is still alive. It is Mr. *Reginald* Mason to whom you are to be married. Their son."

Annabelle went very still. If there

was any more blood to drain out of her head, it did so at that moment. There was a slight ringing in her ears. The air in her nostrils felt cold. She clenched her hands, digging her fingernails painfully into her tingling palms, willing herself not to collapse in an insensible heap at their feet.

"You think to marry me to Mr. *Reginald* Mason?" she asked, staring at her father.

Because he was rich. Or his father was, anyway. There could be no other possible reason. Papa's hatred of Mr. Mason was almost an obsession.

Her father's smile was grim.

"A coalminer's son," he said. "Expensively educated but with coal dust clogging his veins. A wild young rogue, with a reputation for unbridled extravagance and vicious depravity.

48

And a mother and father who are vulgarity personified. Mason's one consuming ambition is to wiggle his way into the ranks of the beau monde. And while he has not been able to accomplish that goal on his own account even after thirty years or more of trying, now at last he has seen an opportunity for his son and has not hesitated to seize it. You may be ruined, Annabelle, but you are still the daughter of the Earl of Havercroft. You are still *Lady* Annabelle Ashton. You are still a prize worth having to someone of Mason's ilk. And he is prepared to pay very dearly indeed for such a soiled trophy."

Annabelle gathered her aristocratic dignity about her and raised disdainful eyebrows — as well as her nose and her chin. She even managed a hollow laugh.

"I hope," she said, "you sent him on his way faster than he came, Papa."

Her mother sniffled.

Her father fixed her with a stony stare.

"What I *did*," he said, "was accept the offer. I had no choice. *You* took away my choices. Mason will be coming again tomorrow with his son for the offer to be formally made — and accepted. *By you.*"

The ringing in Annabelle's ears was turning fuzzy.

"I'll not do it," she whispered. "I'll not do it. You cannot make me. I l-love Thomas."

Her father's voice was like thunder.

"You will never mention that name in this house again," he bellowed.

"But you are quite right about one thing. I cannot force you. I *can*, however, send you to Meadow Hall tomorrow and have you earn your keep as a chambermaid. I cannot afford your keep there, heaven help me, *and* pay a chambermaid. You surely cannot believe that I am rejoicing over this humiliation, Annabelle. To have young Mason as my son-in-law? To have Mason as your *father-in-law?* To be beholden to him for saving me from my difficulties and you from ruin? To know that my peers will forever laugh behind their hands at me? You will listen to young Mason's proposal tomorrow — and you will accept it."

"Oh, Annabelle," her mother said, taking a step toward her. "He is a handsome young man. And only twenty-five. I daresay he is just sowing his wild oats, as young men do. I daresay he will —"

Her voice trailed off. Her husband had turned on her.

"And how, Ellen," he asked coldly, "do you know what young Mason *looks* like?"

It was an absurd question. Young Mr. Mason had sat within feet of them at church every Sunday when both families were at home in the country. He always leered when Annabelle glanced his way or raised an ironical eyebrow or pursed his lips in a suggestion of a kiss. He was, as her mother had just said, very handsome.

"I will not marry him," Annabelle said quickly. "I do not care how young or handsome he is or how respectable he may become at some time in the future. And I do not care how much his father is prepared to pay. I will not do it."

She could hear her voice shaking.

"They are to come at two o'clock tomorrow afternoon," the earl said. "You have until then to change your mind, Annabelle. The alternative is a life of drudgery at Meadow Hall, provided I do not lose it. If you do not like the idea of marrying young Mason, you have only yourself to blame that it has become not only a possibility but a necessity."

Yes, she did have only herself to blame, Annabelle admitted to herself as he gestured her mother out of the room, followed her without another word, and closed the door behind them. She had made the plan and she had set it in motion, and — well, and here she was. She was to marry Reginald Mason instead of the Marquess of Illingsworth, if her father had his way.

From the frying pan into the fire.

She sank down onto a stool that was conveniently at hand and lowered her forehead to her knees.

It was Reginald Mason instead of the Marquess of Illingsworth or her father's utter ruin.

Gracious heaven, it might have been anyone calling at the house an hour ago. It might even have been the marquess calling to forgive her and make her an offer after all. Instead it had been Mr. Mason, come to purchase her for his son.

2

Seventeen Years Ago

There were always strict rules.

The child never doubted that she was loved even though her parents were often away in London for the Season or at a house party on the country estate of one of their numerous friends. She knew they loved her anyway, as did her elderly nurse, who had been Mama's nurse once upon a time in the dim distant past. She was a happy, secure child.

But of course there were rules, all of which were for her own good and intended to keep her from harm. She must never wander alone farther from the house than the kitchen gardens behind it, for example, or the parterre gardens before it. That particular rule was not terribly irksome since she could occupy herself smelling the flowers or talking to the gardeners or skipping along the graveled walks of the parterres or pretending she was in a maze and hopelessly lost and being stalked by a lion or a bear.

It was a *somewhat* irksome rule, though, for she was an inquisitive as well as an imaginative child, and she often found herself standing still among the flowers or on a graveled walk wondering what lay beyond her little world apart from the driveway that led into the village. She really did not know the answer since Mama did not enjoy the outdoors — at least, not to take *exercise* in — and Nurse had elderly legs that no longer worked well enough to allow her to go exploring.

Nurse also had an elderly tendency to nod off during the afternoons and to stay nodded off for a good, long time. The child had timed her once, watching the big hand on the clock in the nursery. It moved once completely around the face and almost halfway around again before Nurse awoke with a start and a snort and remarked that she must have dozed off for a moment.

When she was five, the child started to use those hours of Nurse's sleep for her great disobedience. She began to explore the land surrounding her house. It was not a *very* great disobedience, she told herself, since she never went beyond the boundary of the park. But those stolen hours were always magical. There was something very enticing about breaking the rules and enjoying a sense of freedom and adventure.

One afternoon while she was thus employed, she discovered a co-conspirator. At least, she assumed that was what he was since surely *all* children were governed by strict rules and there was no sign of either a parent or a nurse with him.

As she was approaching the river that formed the eastern border of the park — a favorite destination of hers because she could lie on her stomach on the bank and watch the fish dart by — she heard a mighty splash and rushed forward, hoping to catch a glimpse of a giant fish leaping in the air.

It was not a fish, however, but a boy, who was climbing out of the water by the time she arrived on the scene, wearing only his drawers. He was white and skinny. He had lots of dark hair, which was plastered to his head and forehead, and eyes that looked black, though they were probably only dark brown.

She recognized him. He was the boy she was strictly forbidden even to look at in church. He was vulgar. But this was not church.

"Oh, dear," she said, coming to an abrupt halt several feet from the bank and him. "Did you fall in?"

For a moment she thought he looked scared at the sound of her voice, but then his eyes found her and moved boldly over her, and he sneered.

"I *dived* in," he said.

And sure enough, when she looked she could see an untidy heap of clothes at the foot of an old tree, which had several broad branches stretching invitingly out over the water.

"Oh," she said, "how splendid of you! Does your papa know that you are in *my* papa's park?"

"It isn't *so* your park," he said rudely and in an accent that was unfamiliar to her ears. It was probably what her father called a vulgar accent. "This is *my* father's land."

It was a pronouncement that made her a little uneasy since, if it was true, then she was being very disobedient indeed. But she knew it was *not* true. The river formed the boundary.

"My papa is on *this* side of the river," she said, "and your papa is on *that* side."

"That's all *you* know," he said, setting his hands on his nonexistent hips. "The river is my father's, and those branches are over the river."

It was an argument that almost convinced her until she remembered that branches did not exist independently of trees.

"But the tree is on this side," she pointed out. "And so are you." He was standing on the bank, indisputably in *their* park.

"Pooh!" he said. "What are you going to do about it, then? Run telling tales to *Papa?*"

"My papa is in London," she said.

"But I would not tell him anyway. Are you going to dive in again? Or did you frighten yourself the first time?"

"Pooh!" he said again. "It wasn't the first time or even the *twenty*-first. And nothing scares me."

And he turned, climbed the tree trunk with his bare feet as though he were a particularly nimble monkey, stepped out onto one of the branches, his arms stretched out to the sides, though he still swayed alarmingly, and then jumped, grasping his knees with both arms as he descended.

There was an almighty splash again. One cold drop landed on the little girl's arm, though she was standing too far back to get soaked.

Fortunately.

"That was very splendid indeed,"

she said admiringly after he had shaken his head like a wet dog and then used his skinny arms to haul himself out onto the bank again.

"I bet *you* couldn't do it," he said, sneering.

"I bet I *could*," she said, stung. "But if I did, I would get my hair wet and Nurse would want to know why. And then she would know that I go exploring in the afternoons while she sleeps, and I would not be able to do it any more."

The boy had his hands on his hips again.

"You have a *nurse*," he said contemptuously.

"I do," she admitted. "Don't *you?*"

He rolled his eyes upward.

"I am *eight* years old," he said. "I will be going to school in the autumn.

I have had a tutor since I was five."

"I will have a governess when I am six," she said.

"To teach you *painting* and *embroidery*," he said with undisguised scorn.

"You are the Mason boy," she said. "And you talk strangely."

"And you are the Ashton chit," he said. "And you talk as though you had a plum in your mouth."

"You are rude and horrid," she told him. "I don't think I like you."

"Should I weep?" he asked her, pulling a silly face.

She poked out her tongue and shook her head from side to side, which was a dreadfully unladylike thing to do, but she had been severely provoked.

"I bet," he said, "you couldn't even climb the tree."

"Well, there you are wrong," she said, eyeing it with considerable misgiving. But she had her pride even if she *was* only five, and she was not going to let this nasty, vulgar boy have the final word.

She strode over to the tree, considered removing her shoes and stockings since the leather of the former might get scuffed and the silk of the latter might acquire holes. But she did not like the thought of her bare feet against the rough bark. She did remove her spencer, though, since it might get in the way, and her bonnet, which might impede her vision. She folded the spencer neatly and set it down on the grass close to the untidy heap of the boy's garments, and centered her bonnet carefully on top of it.

"Mind you don't get a crease or a speck of dirt on them," the boy jeered.

Annabelle turned her head and eyed him severely.

"Did your Mama never teach you manners?" she asked, and she proceeded on her way up the tree without waiting for an answer.

It really was not very difficult at all, except when she glanced downward to see how far she had come. She almost froze with terror, but could not do so because the boy was sure to be watching. She did not look down again, though. She looked steadily upward. And her little taste of disobedience during the afternoons must have made her bold, for she did not stop, as she might have done, beside the branch from which the boy had dived. It was not good enough simply to prove that she dared go as high as he had gone. He had annoyed her. She suspected that he had sneered for two particular reasons: that she was a girl and that she was five years old. And so she continued on her way upward, and when she came to another broad branch, she sat on it and edged outward until she felt rather than saw that she was right over the water.

Which, she sensed, was far, far below.

She had probably never been more frightened in her life. In fact, she was sure of it. Never even *half* as frightened.

And that horrid boy was down there somewhere all ready to gloat if she started to cry.

"You see?" she called with quavery gaiety and almost fell off the branch when she risked a downward glance to make sure he was still there to observe her triumph. He was standing where she had left him, his hands still on his hips, his head tilted back.

He was grinning.

"Good enough," he said. "But I bet you can't get down again."

She felt the sudden conviction that he was perfectly right.

She laughed and swung her legs. Her dress must have ridden partway up them when she was moving along the branch. She could feel cool air blow against them.

"You have pluck," he conceded. "I'll give you that."

Which was the first grudging approval he had offered her.

Perhaps she liked him just a little bit after all.

"Jumping is the quickest way down," he called.

The very thought of jumping made her stomach muscles clench convulsively.

She laughed and swung her legs again.

"Then Nurse would find out I had been here, and she would tell Mama and Papa, and I would never be able to come again," she said. "I would never see you again."

"Now wouldn't *that* be a pity?" he said, but when she risked another look down, she could see that he was grinning, not sneering. And he was coming toward the tree and shinning up it, all nimble arms and legs and bare feet.

He stopped at the branch below hers and walked along it, as he had done before, until he was directly below. He tilted back his head and grinned at her yet again.

"We could jump together," he suggested.

Annabelle was feeling a most inconvenient and almost irresistible urge to use the commode.

"You do not care if I am never allowed to come here to see you again, do you?" she said severely. "Because I am a *girl.* And because I am *five.* And because I am the Ashton chit. I am Annabelle."

He reached up his skinny right hand.

"Reggie," he said. "And you're plucky for a girl, Anna, and one who is little more than a baby at that. Let me help you down."

It was rash to refuse such an offer. But she had been stung by the accusation of being little more than a baby, though he had not said it with his customary scorn. Besides, she did not know how she would release her tight hold of her branch in order to take his offered hand.

"I do not need help, thank you all the same," she said.

He grinned yet again, shrugged, turned, and jumped.

Annabelle felt a veritable shower of cold drops on her legs this time. She also felt that she would surely disgrace herself if she did not get to a commode *right now* or even sooner. But she would die if she did disgrace herself. She would never again be able to steal even the merest glance at him in church.

The boy — Reggie — stretched out on the bank to dry, his hands clasped behind his head, and quite deliberately ignored her.

Annabelle did not afterward know how long it took her to inch her way back along the branch and down the trunk. But it was long enough to make her feel panic lest Nurse be awake and aware that she was not in any of the many places in or close to the house where she might legitimately be.

That panic, in addition to the dreadful fear of falling or disgracing herself in other ways, was *not* a comfortable feeling, and long before her feet were on blessedly firm ground again Annabelle was silently promising an unidentified being that if she could only get safely home, she would never, *never* leave it unchaperoned again.

Reggie was leaning nonchalantly against the trunk as she set first one foot and then the other on the ground.

"I'll tell you a secret," he said, "if you promise not to tell anyone else."

"Cross my heart," she said, doing just that with one forefinger.

"I always dive out of the tree," he said, "because I am afraid to climb down."

"No!" she said, thrilled.

"No, not really," he said, shrugging.

"Oh, yes, you are," she said. "And I was afraid too. My legs are still shaking."

She liked his grin. It was a little bit lopsided. His teeth were large and strong-looking, and the front two were ever so slightly crooked.

"So, are you coming again, then?" he asked her.

"I might," she said as he bent and handed her her spencer. He kept hold of her bonnet until she was ready for it.

"Just so that I know never to come here again," he added.

"Suit yourself," she told him. But there was something like a smile in his eyes, and Annabelle laughed out loud.

He laughed back at her.

"We could be friends," she said.

He pulled a face.

"We had better not let anyone know when we go to church," he said.

"I will not look at you at all," she said, "because I am not allowed to.

But when I *do*, I shall look like *this*."

And she borrowed one of her mother's haughtiest expressions. Not that her mother used it often, but Annabelle had always admired it and practiced it frequently before the looking glass in the nursery.

"And I shall look at you like *this*," Reggie said and let his half-closed eyes move slowly and insolently down her body from her head to her toes.

They snorted and giggled together.

"I have to go," she said. "Nurse will be missing me."

And there was a stronger reason than Nurse. She had a hard time not dancing from one foot to the other. She was going to have to stop and squat among the trees as soon as she was out of his sight, even though it would be a dreadfully unladylike thing to do.

"Am I keeping you?" he asked with cool indifference, raising his eyebrows.

She went dashing off for home without retaliating.

Reggie, Reggie, Reggie.

The Mason boy.

Her new friend.

Who was all of eight years old and thought she had *pluck.*

His eyes *were* brown, not black.

3

"You will thank me for this one day, lad," Reggie's father said with hearty good humor as his carriage rocked to a halt outside Havercroft House on Berkeley Square at precisely one minute to two in the afternoon. "Sowing wild oats is one thing, and I paid well enough to educate you in such a way that you were almost bound to sow them just like any other young gentleman. But excessive extravagance is not the way to make or preserve a fortune. The best thing for that is a good and prudent woman, like your mother."

"And like Lady Annabelle Ashton?" Reggie raised his eyebrows.

"Oh, Bernie," his mother said — yes, she was with them too for this historic first-ever visit through the front door of an earl's residence. Reggie feared this was going to be an excruciatingly public offer of marriage. "Lady Annabelle has always been as pretty as any picture, and she and Reginald will make a handsome couple. But are you quite, quite sure about this? How do we know she is not pining for the young man who tried to elope with her? Though it does sound as if he is not worthy of her if he would abandon her without a fight. How do we know that she has any part of her heart left to give our Reginald?"

"She is a fortunate young lady," Reggie's father replied, still beaming with genial triumph, "that Reginald is willing to have her. He is good at heart, as we both know, though what has got into him lately, I do *not* know. It seems rather late in the day for wild oats. Never mind about love, though, Sadie. That will come in time. Not that either of them deserves it, mind you."

"*Willing* may not be quite the right word, sir," Reggie muttered just as the coachman opened the carriage door and set down the steps.

"Oh, I *wish*, Reginald," his mother said, "you would not call your father *sir*, just like a gentleman with no warmth of family affection in his heart."

"I am sorry, Ma," Reggie said, smiling apologetically at her. "I'll call him Da as if I were still an infant, then, shall I?"

"You will always be my little boy," she said sadly. "I shall weep if you ever start calling me *ma'am.*"

Reggie vaulted out of the carriage and offered his hand to help her down. Then he hugged her tightly.

"Ma," he said, "why would I do that? If I ever do, you may clip me about the head, not weep."

She took his father's arm and looked apprehensively toward the house. She appeared to have shrunk to half her size since they left home, whereas his father seemed to have expanded to twice his. All of his thunderous ill-humor of two days ago had fled without a trace. Reggie took a deep breath and expelled it slowly.

This was it, then. A liveried footman, complete with white wig rolled crisply at the sides, was holding open the door of the mansion where Reggie's doom was to be sealed.

They were soon in pursuit of the stiff back of the Havercroft butler, who led them up a broad, impressive staircase to the drawing room. This, Reggie thought as the butler announced them and stood aside, must be the very depth of degradation for Havercroft. The *drawing* room, no less, for his enemy the coal merchant and his family!

There were three people in the room, all of them on their feet or in the process of rising. The earl stood before the cold marble fireplace, his feet slightly apart, his hands clasped at his back, his thin face looking haughty and aristocratic and beaked. He looked as if it might have taken wild horses to drag him there, though he was immaculately turned out, as always. The countess was slender and handsome and smiling. It was a *gracious* smile rather than a warm one, it was true, and therefore perhaps a little condescending, but it was a smile nonetheless.

And then there was Lady Annabelle, who was tricked out for the occasion in white muslin, which almost exactly matched her complexion. Her very blond hair, arranged in elaborate curls about her head and wispy ringlets over her ears, looked almost colorful in comparison. If she had said *boo,* she might have been mistaken for a ghost and they might all have run screaming from the room.

Her face wore no smile, gracious or otherwise. Nor any other expression. She gazed straight ahead at nothing in particular.

Dash it all, she looked as if she had been *suffering*. As no doubt she had.

The sound of Reggie's father rubbing his large hands together was loud in the room for a moment after the butler had finished saying his piece and had closed the door behind the visitors. And then the countess moved gracefully in their direction, both her hands extended toward them — or rather, toward his mother, at whom her smile was directed.

"Mrs. Mason," she said, "I am delighted you have come too. Mothers are excluded all too often from such happy events as this, and really we ought not to be, ought we, since we are the ones who bore and nurtured our children."

"Exactly what I always say," Reggie's mother said, beaming happily as she set her hands in those of the countess and visibly relaxed. "It is even worse when the child is a son, Lady Havercroft. A man always thinks a son is *his*, just as if he appeared from nowhere one day and a woman just happened to be hovering in the next room waiting to provide milk and be called *Ma* and otherwise be ignored. I insisted on coming today. 'Bernie,' I said when I knew he and Reginald were coming, 'I am going too and there is no point in trying to stop me.' "

She sounded breathless by the time she had finished.

"Women!" Reggie's father said genially, looking for confirmation of his good-natured complaint from the earl.

Havercroft offered no such confirmation, and Reggie's father set about rubbing his hands together again.

"Do have a seat," the countess said. "We are pleased to see you, Mr. Mason. And you too, Mr. Reginald Mason."

Lady Annabelle Ashton sank back into the seat from which she had risen on their arrival. It was as close to one of the windows as it could be without actually falling out of it to the ground below.

Reggie sat some distance from her. He would have lifted one hand to loosen the knot of his neckcloth, but such a gesture would suggest that he did not feel entirely comfortable, and he did not want to give anyone the satisfaction of suspecting that that was true.

"Mr. Mason," the countess said, her eyes on him, "have you met my daughter? Annabelle, make your curtsy to Mr. Reginald Mason, if you please."

Reggie jumped back to his feet as Lady Annabelle got to hers.

"Lady Annabelle," he said, making her a bow.

"Mr. Mason," she said, curtsying.

All of which was utterly absurd. They had lived less than two miles from each other most of their lives, both of them under strict orders to ignore the very existence of the other. Now they were finally being introduced and expected to *marry*.

Her eyes did not quite meet his as

she resumed her seat and he felt permitted to resume his. Her jaw was set in a hard line. He wondered what was going through her mind.

His father was openly looking about the room, doubtless pricing out every item down to the last penny and concluding with great satisfaction that the Havercroft drawing room, for all its brocaded walls and gilded frieze and landscape originals in their heavy gold frames, was no more expensive than their own.

Lady Havercroft began a polite conversation about the weather and the health of the king and the hot air balloon that had ascended from Hyde Park last week. Reggie's mother hoped the weather would stay warm for the summer in the country, though they needed some rain, of course, to keep the grass green and grow the crops, and anyway it was greedy to ask for too much good weather. And pointless too since the weather did what it pleased no matter what they wished. Which was a good thing since everyone wanted different weather for different reasons and might end up fighting wars over it if they were able to control it. As if there were not enough things already to fight wars over. His father pronounced flat out that the king was mad, which was a pity since the Prince Regent was even more of an idiot, and that if men had been meant to fly, the good Lord would surely have given them wings. And some men were filled with enough hot air without there being more beneath their feet — an observation that was followed by a hearty and unilateral bellow of laughter.

The shadow of a smile flitted across Lady Annabelle's ghost-pale lips.

It was many months since Reggie had seen his father so brimful of good humor.

"Well," his father said at last, breaking a short silence that threatened to become awkward, "I have brought Reginald to make his offer to your daughter, Havercroft, according to our agreement yesterday. Shall we hear him do it so that the whole business can be sealed up right and tight?"

The earl turned steely gray eyes upon Reginald. He might have regarded a worm beneath his boot with more respect and less dislike.

"I could hardly have phrased it better myself," he said, his tone quiet and aristocratic and withering.

Reggie's father did not wither. He rubbed his hands and beamed.

"Get to it, then, lad," he said.

Right! A public offer it was to be, then, both sets of parents watching and listening and judging. How utterly delightful!

Should he stand? Sit? *Kneel?* Move closer? Farther away? All the way out onto the landing? Should he smile? Frown? Look contrite? Amorous? Grateful? Humble? Dignified? Triumphant? Defeated? Defiant? Compliant? Supercilious?

Good Lord, his mind was babbling, and he was missing what the Countess of Havercroft was saying. She had risen to her feet to say it, and Reggie scrambled to his again.

"Mr. Mason, William," she said, looking from Reggie's father to Havercroft, "how can you possibly expect the young people to come to any sort of amicable agreement unless they are given the chance to speak privately with each other? We will leave them alone. Mrs. Mason, do come into the music room. I will have tea fetched there."

And she swept across the room and opened a door that led to a connecting room — the music room, obviously. Reggie glimpsed a large pianoforte in there and his mother exclaimed over its size. The two older men followed, one behind the other. The earl was the last through the door. Reggie waited for it to shut.

He waited in vain. It closed, but only halfway.

Privacy, it seemed, was to be illusory.

There was no sound of conversation from beyond the door. They had probably all pulled up chairs to listen. And also to watch? It was impossible to tell.

He turned his head to look at Lady Annabelle. She was also looking at the door — and then at him. Their eyes locked and held.

He raised his eyebrows. She raised hers. She was far better at it than he. Her eyebrows had been born aristocratic.

"Well," he said.

"Well," she replied.

Mr. Bernard Mason was huge. His head was as round as a large ball and almost as bald. It had glistened in the sunlight that was streaming through the drawing room windows. He had an amiable, almost jovial face. He spoke with a broad north country accent.

Mrs. Mason was plump and pretty. She seemed placid and good-natured. She spoke with the same accent.

Both were talkative. Both were absolutely appalling in her father's eyes. Annabelle had been able to see that. The fact that he was beholden to them, that he must marry her, his only daughter, to their son, must be the stuff of nightmares to him.

But he was not the one who was going to have to marry Mr. Reginald Mason.

Annabelle liked his parents. She always had. Not that she had been allowed to have any dealings whatsoever with them, but she had not been able to help hearing Mr. Mason's booming voice when he talked with the vicar after church, or his loud laugh when he exchanged pleasantries with fellow parishioners. And once, when she and her mama had taken a basket of food to a sick villager, sitting in their carriage until their coachman had delivered the offering and the woman of the house had come out to make her curtsy and shower them with thanks, the woman had remarked that Mrs. Mason had called earlier and had sat talking with the sick person for all of half an hour. Annabelle had wished that *they* had done that. It sounded like fun. It sounded compassionate.

Their son was a different matter altogether. Although he bore a faint resemblance to his mother, it was really so faint as to be virtually non-existent. He was dark-haired and tall and slender, with broad shoulders, a narrow waist and hips, and long, well-muscled legs. He was immaculately tailored and elegant. He spoke with the refined accent of a gentleman. And his face, faultlessly handsome, was set in an expression that seemed halfway between amusement and contempt.

How dare he!

"It would seem," he said when it became obvious to both of them that the door between the drawing room and the music room was not going to be shut, "that our fathers between them have arranged our marriage, Lady Annabelle."

He did not bother to lower his voice

or disguise the fact that the idea had not been his.

"Yes," she said, gazing at him disdainfully. If he was going to look at her *that* way, then she was going to look back at him *this* way.

"And yet," he said, "only a week ago you were so determined to marry someone else that you ran off with him. Your father's coachman, I understand."

She pressed her lips together and glared at him. Her eyes narrowed. Oh, he was going to play games with her, was he?

"What was his name?" he asked.

"Thomas Till," she said. "I would guess it still *is* his name."

"*Till?*" His mouth quirked at one corner. "You would have enjoyed being Mrs. Annabelle *Till?*"

"Far more than I will enjoy being Mrs. Annabelle *Mason,* I daresay," she retorted, forgetting for a moment that they had an audience beyond the music room doors.

He inclined his head slightly in acknowledgment of the hit, and his eyes dared to laugh.

"You lament his departure from your life, then?" he asked her.

She glanced toward the half-open door, remembering.

"My decision to elope was a mistake," she said disdainfully. "It was rash and impulsive."

"You are impulsive by nature, then?" he asked her. "And rash? And fickle?"

Oh.

Oh!

Annabelle's nostrils flared and she

glared. He looked politely back at her as though he had asked her if she would like some tea.

From beyond the door into the music room there was a male throat-clearing followed by a female murmuring. And then silence.

Well, two could play his game. Her eyes narrowed.

"I understand, Mr. Mason," she said, "that you are *extravagant.*"

His eyebrows, which had returned to their normal place above his eyes a few moments ago, arched upward again.

"It is a deadly sin indeed," he said, "and I am guilty as charged."

"I have heard," she said, "that you need a whole extra *room* for all your clothes since your dressing room is not large enough to accommodate them all. And that your gambling debts are high enough to finance a small country for a decade. Are you weak-willed by nature? And irresponsible? And foppish?"

There was a distinct male chuckle from the next room followed by a female shushing and silence.

He stared long and hard at her, his lips pursed.

"How small a country are we talking about here?" he asked. "I fear your informant may be prone to exaggeration — which is really quite unusual for a gossip. *Half* a decade may be more accurate. Perhaps three-quarters. But should we reserve the insults for later, after we are married? Our parents must be waiting with some anxiety to hear the outcome of this *private* encounter."

"I beg your pardon," she said haughtily, lifting her chin and looking at him along the length of her nose, "but is it not premature to refer to the time *after we are married?* I have not heard you offer me marriage yet. And I certainly have not accepted that offer."

"But you will," he said. "Hear my offer and accept it, that is. You really have no choice, do you? Till is probably halfway across the American Wild West by now and still running."

"I have exactly as much choice as you," she said. "A man's debtors can become rather nasty, I have heard, when his father is not forthcoming with the funds to pay them."

He nodded slowly for a few silent moments.

"Touché," he said. "Ours is sure to

be a match made in heaven, I see. We will doubtless live happily ever after. Is there another cliché to better describe the bliss of our future union?"

"A love to outlast all loves?" she suggested. "A melding of souls for all eternity?"

"There is no need to exaggerate," he said crisply, and he came striding toward her across the room until he was only a foot or so away.

Annabelle had to tip back her head slightly to look into his face. She could smell his cologne, feel his body heat. She swallowed and then wished she had not. The sound of it seemed to fill the room.

He seemed very large and . . . *virile.*

"Tell me, Lady Annabelle," he said, "do you still have tender feelings for Till?"

She narrowed her eyes at him again.

"I do," she said, "And tell me, Mr. Mason, do you need all those clothes you purchased?"

"I do," he said, one corner of his mouth lifting in a mocking smile. "Especially the boots. Ten pairs in the last ten weeks if memory serves me correctly, each more fashionable than the last. You look more becoming with color in your cheeks and light in your eyes. You looked like a ghost when I arrived with my parents."

Was *that* why he had been so obnoxious? To bring a flush to her cheeks and a spark to her eyes?

And then his voice dropped so low that she scarcely heard what he said.

"Do you suppose they can see as well as hear?"

"Possibly," she said just as softly.

He pursed his lips again.

"We will proceed to business, then," he said, his voice at normal volume again and brisk and businesslike.

He took her right hand in his — which was warm in contrast with her own — and he . . .

Oh, yes, he really did. He went down on one knee before her.

"Lady Annabelle," he said, looking up at her, his very dark eyes soulful, almost worshipful, and surely many fathoms deep, "will you do me the great honor of marrying me and making me the happiest of men?"

She could not stop herself from feeling a great welling of emotion. She had always dreamed of such a moment. What woman did not? And here it was. But it was a *public* moment even though their parents were hidden from sight, and this was all a charade, performed for their benefit.

"I will," she said. And she said it softly, for him only. If they wanted to hear it in the music room, let them strain their ears.

He lifted her hand to his lips, and she felt the pressure of them against her fingers and the warmth of his breath against the back of her hand. There was a soreness in her throat as she fought — foolishly — against the tears that threatened.

This was not right. This was *really* not right.

Which was probably the understatement of the century.

And yet . . . Oh, and yet . . .

He did not even have time to look up or get to his feet before the music room door opened fully and their parents surged back into the drawing room, Papa looking stern and perhaps relieved, Mr. Mason smiling broadly and rubbing his hands together, Mrs. Mason smiling happily, and Mama's eyes glistening with unshed tears — though she was smiling too.

Her answer must have been audible after all, Annabelle thought a moment before Mr. Mason grasped the hand of his son, now back on his feet, and pumped it heartily up and down, while Mrs. Mason folded Annabelle to her ample bosom.

"My dear Lady Annabelle," she said, "I have always dreamed of having a daughter, though nature denied me any other child but Reginald. And now I am to have one after all. No daughter will ever have been welcomed into a family more warmly than you will be into ours. Oh, except by your mama, that is. I am sure *she* has always made a fuss of you. You were always as pretty as a picture, even as a very little girl. Oh, my dear, I am so *happy* I could weep. And you will be happy too, mark my words, even if you may doubt it now. Reginald has been somewhat wild lately, but he has always been a good-hearted, affectionate boy."

And then Annabelle found herself being folded to the large chest of her future father-in-law and kissed noisily on one cheek and called daughter.

Finally her mother hugged her tightly and wordlessly.

Her father was standing before the fireplace again as if he had not moved since the sound of carriage wheels outside in the square had announced the arrival of the Masons.

"The betrothal announcement will be in tomorrow's papers, and the first banns will be called at St. George's on Sunday," he said when everyone else had stopped hugging and kissing and laughing — those last two activities exclusive to the elder Masons. "On Monday there will be a betrothal ball here. Everyone will come, curiosity being the dominant characteristic of the *ton.* You will be saved from ruin, Annabelle, and you, Mason, will be elevated in rank by your marriage. Everyone will be satisfied that justice has been done and respectability preserved, and in one month's time, after your nuptials, you may live together for the rest of your lives as best you may."

No mention of the fact that his own financial ruin had just been averted.

"Happily ever after, I am sure," Mrs. Mason said, beaming.

"The Masons have always enjoyed long, grand marriages," Mr. Mason said, rubbing his hands in what Annabelle realized was a habitual gesture when he was pleased. "We know a thing or two about loving, eh, Sadie?"

"I am quite sure, William," Mama said with quiet dignity, "Annabelle and Mr. Reginald Mason *will* make the best of their marriage. I am hopeful that they will."

"Hope costs nothing," Papa said.

And all the while Reginald Mason stood a few feet from Annabelle and said not a word. Neither did she. He was looking at her with steady, unreadable eyes. She glanced at him but could not hold his gaze.

She should perhaps be smiling. But everything in her wanted to weep. She was not quite sure why.

She glanced at her betrothed again. Her *betrothed.* He looked back but said nothing.

She was going to be Lady Annabelle Mason.

Mrs. Reginald Mason.

It had all been accomplished in a twenty-four-hour period.

All sewn up right and tight.

4

Ten Years Ago

The youth sprawled on the bank of the river was sucking on a blade of grass. He was feeling relaxed and sleepy in the heat of the summer sun. He half listened to the song of some unidentified bird hidden in the trees behind him and gazed up with half-closed eyes at the few small, fluffy white clouds that were scudding across the sky, blown by a wind that did not reach the ground.

A slight breeze would feel rather pleasant, but he would not move into the shade. He liked being just here.

It had been a favorite haunt of his as a child, even though technically he had been trespassing here, as he was now. It was Oakridge land. Why it should have always been more attractive to him than the land on the other side of the river a mere few yards away he did not know. Or perhaps he did. The other side belonged to his father. There was not that titillating feeling of danger there.

And of course the old oak tree was on this side.

He turned his head to look at it. It still looked rather impressive even through his fifteen-year-old eyes: large and solid and ancient. It had been a child's paradise. He had climbed it nimbly and endlessly as a boy — once he had conquered his fear of heights, that is. He had often sat in its branches, weaving imaginative tales in which he was a pirate or a highwayman or Robin Hood or a knight on the ramparts of his castle, the moat below and a horde of fierce barbarian attackers massed on his father's side of the water.

He had always ended up diving into the river, for he had never quite overcome his terror of climbing *down* the tree.

Besides, diving was a thrilling, dangerous thing to do.

It was a long time since he was last here. He had come for a few years, even after he went away to school, but for some unremembered reason he had stopped, and then he had forgotten all about this place. Until today, that was, when he had been wandering aimlessly about the perimeter of his father's park.

Actually it was quite rare for him to be at home. He was away at school most of the time, and during holidays he was often invited to spend a few weeks with school friends at their country homes. And his parents — his father anyway — liked to travel and took him all over the British Isles during his holidays — and even to Europe when a lull in the wars allowed foreign travel.

It felt good to be home.

He dozed off for a minute or two, but it was not a deep sleep. He was aware of the world around him at the same time as he floated pleasantly on the surface of a fuzzy slumber. He heard the horse approaching.

He woke up fully and opened his eyes.

What now? Should he lie quietly here and hope horse and rider would pass on by without seeing him, as would probably happen? Or should he make a dive for the river and the safety of his own side of it?

That latter course of action would have been a great indignity even to his childhood self. It was unthinkable to his almost-adult pride. Besides, he was fully clothed, having crossed the river higher up, where it was narrower and there were enough large stones embedded in it to form a precarious sort of bridge.

He stayed where he was and relaxed into what he hoped would look like nonchalance if he *was* caught.

The horse drew closer, and closer

yet. And then stopped.

Drat it, he had been spotted.

Reggie sucked on his grass stem and gazed up into the branches of the tree as though he were deaf.

"Oh," a female voice said, sounding both surprised and delighted. "Hello."

He knew immediately who she was, and it came to him in a rush that he had stopped coming here when *she* had. She had not been caught here with him — a disaster that would have had dire consequences for both of them — but she *had* been caught farther from the house than she was allowed to go alone, even though she must have been six or seven at the time. She had been more carefully guarded after that.

They had been childhood friends.

They had not met often, it was true, but they *had* met. At first he had barely tolerated her but had insulted and teased and scowled at her. It had seemed beneath his eight-year-old dignity, after all, to have a five-year-old *girl* as a friend. But she had been a plucky, cheerful little thing — and a daring one too. Though she had never dived into the river, purely for the reason that she would get her hair wet and so betray her truancy when she returned home, she *had* climbed both up and down the oak tree and joined in all his games. She had steadfastly refused to be a damsel in distress, though. She had been his right-hand man in all his exploits. She had sometimes demanded that *he* be *her* right-hand man, but she had never won those battles. He had taught her to fish, and she had had a knack for catching them. Her gender had always betrayed her when she reeled them in, though. She had always detached the hook with swift tenderness and placed the fish gently back in the water. When he had jeered at her, she had stuck out her tongue at him and crossed her eyes.

He sat up now and turned toward her.

"You have managed to escape all your nurses?" he asked with contempt in his voice.

"You are still a trespasser?" she countered haughtily.

She was dressed very fashionably in a bright blue riding habit with an absurd little hat sitting on her blond curls and tipped over one eyebrow. She was as thin as a reed, and very pretty if one liked flat-chested chits. Reggie did not. He liked just the opposite.

"You are going to run and tell tales to Papa?" he asked her.

"He would wonder if I had discovered it while gazing into a crystal ball in the schoolroom," she said. "I would not tell him anyway, even if I could do it without betraying myself. I am not a tattle-tale. What are you doing here?"

"Eating your father's grass," he said, tossing the blade aside, "and enjoying the solitude. At least, I *was* enjoying it."

"I saw you at church last Sunday," she told him.

"I thought you weren't supposed to look," he said.

Her pert little nose had been stuck

in the air as she had pointedly *not* looked his way.

"I did not look," she said. "I *heard* you, singing the hymns. Off key."

Which was a horrible bouncer. He had not opened his mouth.

"You did not," he said and scowled at her.

"All the *other* girls were looking at you," she said. "They think you are ever so gorgeous."

She laughed, and it was a bright, merry sound, not the sort of female giggle that grated on male ears.

"As long as *you* don't," he said.

"I would think not," she said tartly. "If you keep looking at people like that, you are going to grow into Mr. Gruff-and-Grim by the time you are twenty, and no one will think you gorgeous at all. Help me down."

It was an order issued with the aristocratic assumption that he would run to obey.

"Maybe," he said rudely, "I don't want your company."

"Then go back to your *own* park," she said. "Help me down."

He got to his feet and strolled reluctantly toward her. If he remembered correctly, she was three years younger than he. What self-respecting man of his age was interested in a *twelve*-year-old?

But she was not quite flat-chested, he discovered when he lifted her down from her sidesaddle. Her breasts were budding. They were almost invisible to the eye, at least through the fabric of her habit. But he could *feel* them when she came hurtling downward rather too fast and rubbed against him all the way to the ground.

"Oops," she said and laughed.

"Oops," he said simultaneously and . . . dash it all, he hoped he was not *blushing.* He scowled again.

She was a tiny little thing. She reached barely to his shoulder. Of course, he had had a growth spurt in the last three or four months. If she was going to have one, it had not happened yet. She looked like a child, even if she did not quite *feel* like one.

Dash it, but the fellows at school would pour endless ridicule upon him if they could see him now, spending a precious holiday afternoon with a stick of a *girl.*

"I have not been here for *ages,*" she said.

"Me neither."

"You have not been diving today," she said. "Your hair is dry."

"Diving out of trees is for *children*," he said.

"And you are not a child any longer," she said tipping her head to one side so that the feather in her little hat brushed one of her shoulders. "No, I can see you are not. And you are not a pirate or a sea captain or a Viking warrior any longer. Those were good days, were they not? Come and sit down again. Tell me about yourself."

"The horse?" he said, indicating it.

"Pegasus?" she said and laughed. "Have you heard a less imaginative name for a horse? Or a less suitable one? He is as meek as a mouse. He will graze quietly here until I am ready to go home."

And she sat down on the grass close to the bank, removed the pins from her hat and tossed it aside, raised her knees, and arranged her skirts about her legs before clasping her arms about them. She rested one cheek against her knees and gazed across at him as he sat cross-legged beside her.

"I have missed those days when we were children," she said. "I have missed *you,* Reggie."

She sounded wistful. How could he tell her that he had forgotten all about those days and about her until she had come riding up?

Her lips curved into a smile and her eyes danced with merriment.

"You had forgotten my very existence, had you not?" she said. "Boys are horrid, careless creatures. But then, of course, you have more with which to fill your heads than we do. You go to school, and I daresay you have dozens of friends. You must have, for sometimes your mama and papa are here and you are not even though it is between school terms. Tell me about school."

He shrugged.

"It is a crashing bore," he said.

She tutted. "There is something about boys," she said, "that makes them think it is unmanly to show any feelings other than scorn and irritation or any enthusiasm for anything. It is a very unattractive trait."

"I am not trying to attract you," he said.

There was a short silence.

"Do you want me to go away?" she asked. "I will if you wish. Even though it is *you* who are trespassing."

He turned his head to look at her. She really was a pretty little thing. At this moment she was all large, wistful blue eyes.

"Anna," he said, and then felt very foolish because he had nothing else to say. He had forgotten that he used to call her that because *Annabelle* seemed altogether too girly.

She smiled.

"You are the only person who has ever called me that," she said. "Do you remember the day I climbed up the tree and must have taken an hour or more to climb down again? I have never been more terrified in my life."

He did remember actually. He remembered wondering, with knees that threatened to knock together, if he was going to have to be a real-life hero and climb back up to her rescue.

But she had done it on her own without once demanding or pleading for assistance.

"I remember," he said.

"You told me I had pluck," she said. "It was the loveliest compliment I had ever been paid. Perhaps it still is."

She laughed.

"You used to catch fish," he said, "and throw them back in. Just like a *girl.*"

"I *am* a girl," she said, and their eyes locked.

He felt a return of that discomfort he had felt when he lifted her awkwardly from her horse and felt her body rub along his as she descended. A slight hotness. A slight breathlessness.

Over a shapeless *girl* who stuck her

nose in the air when she saw him at church.

There was a spot of color in her left cheek, the only one that was visible to him. It suggested that she was suddenly uncomfortable too.

"I'll race you to the top of the tree," she said.

"That's *children's* stuff," he said scornfully.

But she had jumped to her feet and darted to the oak tree. She started to climb, and he had a brief view of thin legs encased in riding boots and the white shift beneath her riding habit.

He watched her for a few moments. He hoped she was not going to get stuck halfway up or, worse, at the top. He hoped she was not going to wail down at him to come to her rescue.

But he knew she would not. She would rescue herself. He sensed that she had not changed in that way.

He despised himself for still liking her.

How the fellows would laugh.

He went after her.

They climbed in silence for a while, until she started to laugh — a light, exuberant sound. He laughed too and found a different route to the top so that he could overtake her.

They met well above the branches where they had played as young children. She eased herself down to a sitting position between the trunk and a slightly upward-sloping branch, and he stood on a branch to one side of hers, one arm wrapped about the trunk. They were enclosed by wood and leaves. Beyond there was the blue of the sky and the answering blue of the river below.

"Are you scared?" she asked him.

"No."

"Liar!"

"Are you?" he asked.

"No."

"Liar!"

They both snorted at the silliness, and he lowered himself gingerly until he was sitting on his branch, his knees drawn up. Their shoulders almost touched.

"How are we going to get down?" she asked, and laughed again.

"Perhaps we will have to live the rest of our lives up here," he said.

"I hope not," she told him. "If I am not back within the hour there is going to be one very anxious groom in our stables. He is supposed to ride behind me at all times, but I have persuaded him that he does not need to do so when I have promised not to leave the park. I think he chooses to believe the suggestion came from my father but suspects it did not."

He turned his head and looked at her profile. She still had a child's face. Though that was not quite right. She looked different from the round-cheeked little girl with whom he used to play. She was going to be a beautiful woman when she had grown a bit and developed breasts and hips and all their accompanying curves. She would probably marry a duke or a marquess or an earl. Perhaps even a prince.

Sometimes he resented the fact that he was not of her class and never would be for all his schooling and his father's wealth.

Not that he wanted her to marry *him.*

She turned her head too, and he was caught gazing at her.

She smiled.

"Reggie," she said, "tell me about school. Tell me about *you.* I have heaps of cousins and friends and acquaintances. But I have never forgotten you."

It amazed him that she would so easily open herself to rejection and scorn. He would never admit such a thing to her, even if it were true. Perhaps that was one fundamental difference between males and females.

But . . . she had never forgotten him?

"School is jolly good fun, actually,"

he said.

"Is it?"

And he found himself telling her stories of school and the masters and his fellow pupils. He chose anecdotes that would make her laugh. He told her about his travels with his parents, about the Lake District and the Scottish Highlands and Mount Snowdon and Harlech Castle in North Wales. He told her about the relatives they visited in the north of England, more numerous, it seemed, than the stars in the sky, all loud and boisterous and affectionate.

And she told him about her governess and her studies and her visits to relatives at their various country homes and to Bath and Bristol. She had him chuckling and even laughing aloud at some of the stories she told.

"Oh, Reggie," she said at last, "it *is* lovely to see you again. I have had more fun this afternoon than I have had all summer."

He could hardly say the same. He had spent a few weeks with one particularly jolly school chum in Cornwall. He had sailed and swum in the sea and climbed cliffs — *up,* not down — and ridden across rugged country and played cricket and done a dozen and one other exciting things.

"Will you come again?" he asked.

"Will *you?*"

"I asked first," he said. And then, in a burst of nobility, "But I will answer first. Yes, I will come again."

"Tomorrow?" she said.

"Perhaps," he said. "If nothing else is planned, or if it does not rain, or if

I feel like it."

"Well, I won't come here *ever* again," she cried, and with a wicked laugh she swung her legs over the branch and began to descend.

She went down as though she had not a nervous bone in her body. She laughed all the way down.

Reggie, feeling foolish and not a little annoyed, went gingerly after her. He went far faster than he would have done if he had been alone. He expelled a long, silent breath when his feet were safely on the ground.

"You must help me mount Pegasus," she said. "If there were a mounting block here I could do it myself, but there is not."

She was back to aristocratic presumption. She did not *ask*. She *told*.

"Yes, miss, whatever you say, miss,"

he said, and he pulled humbly on his forelock.

She turned her head to look at him.

"*That* is what is different," she said. "It has been puzzling me all the time. You just spoke in your lovely accent again, as you used to do. All the rest of the time you have spoken like everyone else I know. *Do* help me up or I will be late."

His implied complaint and insult had completely escaped her. All she had noticed was that he had acquired an upper-class accent.

He cupped his hands when she had hold of the horse, and she set one small boot in them so that he could hoist her upward. She was as light as a feather.

She looked down at him when she was settled in her sidesaddle, the reins gathered in one hand.

"Reggie," she said, "I *will* come again. Maybe not tomorrow, but I *will* come."

And she reached down with her free hand and cupped his cheek with it.

He felt, foolishly, as if he had been scalded. He held his hand to his cheek as he watched her ride away — a stick of a girl with proud bearing and — *no hat.*

"Hey, Anna," he called, and he swept it up and ran to take it to her — just like a lackey.

"Oh, *thank* you, Reggie," she said as she took it and settled it somehow on her curls. "*Someone* would have noticed. You are my knight in shining armor."

And off she rode again.

A knight in shining armor indeed!

Cliché. Child's stuff.

But he felt absurdly pleased.

5

Reggie and his parents were not invited to dine at Havercroft House on the evening of the engagement ball, though there was a dinner for a number of Havercroft's relatives and inner circle of friends. One of Reggie's acquaintances had told him of it.

Reggie was not surprised that they had been excluded. What if his mother slurped her soup, after all, or his father tucked his napkin into the top of his cravat? What if *he* should use his dessert spoon for the fish course or the butter knife to hack at his beef?

Instead they were to attend only the ball, and Havercroft was to propose a toast to his daughter and her betrothed during supper. They were to stand in the receiving line too, something Havercroft must deplore but could hardly avoid without raising eyebrows throughout the *ton.*

Reggie had been to a few *ton* balls, though to none given by any of the most fashionable hostesses, it was true. He had been educated as a gentleman, after all, and most of his friends were of the upper classes.

His parents, however, were about to attend their first such ball. His father was as puffed up about it as that balloon had been with hot air when it lifted off from Hyde Park last week.

His mother, by contrast, was so consumed by the jitters that she scarcely ate or sat down or stopped talking for two days before it. She probably did not sleep either. Reggie's father had borne her off to the modiste with the highest prices and thickest French accent on Bond Street to be decked out in a purple splendor of a gown that was all wrong for her coloring and then on to other exclusive establishments for the trappings of silver slippers, silver hair plumes, silver gloves and fan and reticule, silver chains for her neck and wrists, and silver earrings.

"Ma," Reggie said when he saw her on the evening of the ball, "every other lady ought to be warned to stay at home this evening. You will severely outshine and outclass them all."

He bowed over her gloved hand and raised it to his lips.

"Just what I said, lad," his father said, beaming with genial pride and holding his head very still and very erect so that his high starched shirt points would not pierce his eyeballs. "Your mother gets lovelier with every passing year."

"How silly of you both," she said, jangling metallically as she laughed. "I daresay no one will even notice me among all the fine ladies. I just hope I will not disgrace you, Reginald."

"Disgrace me?" He possessed himself of her other hand and squeezed both tightly. The laughter faded from his eyes. "You could never *ever* do that, Ma, even if you tried. I hope *I* have not disgraced *you.*"

Guilt, he was finding, was a troublesome commodity. He had hurt his mother with his extravagances, and he had made her anxious now when she feared he might be making an unhappy marriage — even when she denied such anxiety.

"Well, Reginald," she said, "I *was* a little disappointed when it seemed that you were turning into a frivolous young man, because you have never before been like that. But I know that I am about to get my son back again the way he used to be. I know this is going to be a good marriage. Lady Annabelle is a lovely young lady, and you make a handsome couple. Don't they, Bernie?"

Ah, the eternal optimism of mothers! He had been wild and extravagant to a fault, surely putting a noticeable dent in even his father's enormous fortune. And his betrothed had run off with another man less than two weeks ago and would, as far as anyone knew, have continued to run all the way to Scotland with him if they had not been pursued so soon and he had not taken fright and leapt through a window, abandoning her to her fate.

This fate, in fact. She was affianced to him.

He kissed the back of one of his mother's plump hands again.

"They do that, Sadie," his father agreed, though he surely must believe otherwise. "It is time to go."

Reggie saw the renewed fright in his mother's eyes and smiled at her before tucking her hand through his arm.

"You will be the belle of the ball,

Ma," he said.

His father followed them out to the carriage. He had recovered his usual good spirits since the betrothal and treated his son with all the old affection, as though it was Reggie who had been responsible for his great good fortune — as, in a sense, he was. For though it was probably costing a king's ransom to secure Lady Annabelle Ashton as Reggie's bride, the reward of being connected at last to the *ton* — and specifically to the Earl of Havercroft's corner of the *ton* — must seem worth the sacrifice of every last guinea.

This ball really ought to be a total disaster, Reggie thought. It should be shunned by simply everyone on the guest list. And, incidentally, he and his parents had not been invited to add any names to that list. But of course it would *not* be a disaster, but rather one of the grandest squeezes of the Season. Scandal was something upon which the *ton* thrived. It drew them like a powerful magnet.

And there was nothing more scandalous — during this particular month, anyway — than the newly betrothed couple. The prospective bride, an earl's only daughter, had eloped with her father's own coachman and had been seen by half the world as she made her escape. And the prospective groom was the idle and extravagant son of a man who had made his fortune in coal and a woman whose father had owned a butcher's shop in some obscure northern town of which no one had ever heard.

The very proud Earl of Havercroft had been brought low indeed — and everyone knew why. His financial woes had been common knowledge. The coal merchant, by contrast, had been raised to lofty heights indeed. So had his son, who was as handsome as Lady Annabelle was beautiful. Everyone must be agog to discover how they would behave toward each other on this occasion.

Oh, everyone would come to the ball right enough. How could anyone possibly resist? Everyone loved an unhappy couple, especially one who was being forced into marriage. How could they *not* be unhappy under the circumstances?

His task tonight, Reggie thought as he handed his mother into the carriage, making sure that she did not snap off her plumes on the top of the doorframe or tread on the heavy brocade of her skirt as she climbed the steps, was to oblige the ball guests and give them the show they had come to see. And to give his father and Havercroft what *they* expected. And to give his mother and Lady Annabelle's as little pain as he possibly could. And to treat his betrothed with just enough civility to avoid censure as a gentleman but not enough ardor to be accused of hypocrisy.

Fortunately, he had been a member of a drama group at university. He was going to need all his acting skills tonight. He was going to be on public display to an alarming degree.

He wondered if his betrothed had retained some of the color he had goaded into her complexion by annoying her the afternoon he proposed to her. If someone had held a stick of chalk up to her cheek before he did so on that occasion it would have faded into invisibility. He hoped that at least she had the good sense to wear something other than white this evening.

He wondered if she was nervous. *He* was, dash it all. Good lord, he was an engaged man. He was going to be married within the month.

It was actually happening.

Annabelle was standing in a receiving line that seemed as if it would never end, with her betrothed at her side. Reginald Mason. She doubted that even a single one of the invitations had been sent in vain. *Everyone* had come, and everyone looked with avid curiosity at the two of them as they passed. His arm was almost brushing her shoulder, though they had scarcely glanced at each other since his arrival with his parents. When she *did* steal a glance, it was to see that he was smiling with all his considerable charm at all and sundry. But then she was smiling too.

They were behaving, as expected, like a happily betrothed couple.

Mrs. Mason was beside her on the other side, her husband beyond her. They were both shaking hands with everyone when a curtsy and a bow would have sufficed, and they both seemed to feel it necessary to chat with everyone and so hold up the progress of the line. It must surely stretch all the way down the stairs and across the hall to the front doors. Maybe even outside the doors. That would cause problems for some footmen and coachmen.

She did not doubt that Papa was severely annoyed by the delay. He was probably feeling horribly humiliated too. Mama was being her usual gracious self. Annabelle suspected that her mother rather liked Mrs. Mason, though she had not said so.

Finally the line came to an end and Mr. Mason stood rubbing his hands together and gazing about genially while his son inclined his head to Annabelle and offered her his arm. He was still smiling and at last he was smiling directly at her. With unreadable eyes.

They were to lead off the dancing. Annabelle felt so exposed when they stepped onto the empty dance floor that she even glanced down to make sure that she really had remembered to put on her gown. Candles flickered brightly from every holder in the candelabra above and from every wall sconce. Banks of white roses and carnations and green ferns had turned the ballroom into a fragrant garden. Guests were crammed three and four deep about the perimeter of the room, a kaleidoscope of color, rich jewels twinkling and sparkling to rival the candles.

Her betrothed settled her a short distance from him and gazed steadily at her as other couples began to form lines beside them. He was no longer smiling. Annabelle frowned slightly at him. Was it not enough that every other eye in the room was on her?

Must his be too — as if he would see right through to the back of her mind? She felt a childish urge to poke her tongue out at him, and she was alarmed lest she actually do it.

"You ought not to have done it," he said, and for a moment she thought that perhaps she really *had* . . .

But he explained what he meant.

"Worn white, that is," he said.

She hated wearing white, but it was what most unmarried young ladies wore, and for a while longer she was an unmarried young lady.

"Mama thought it important that I look . . . well, *innocent,*" she said.

"Virginal?" He raised his eyebrows. "One might as well call a spade a spade, Lady Annabelle. It was probably misguided advice. The less attention you draw to your possibly virginal state the better, would you not agree?"

Her jaw might have dropped if she had not been so aware of all the watching eyes. She glared at him instead. Her nostrils flared.

"There is surely no need to be *offensive*," she said.

"Are you, ah, *virginal?*" he asked.

She felt suddenly as if two candles must have dropped from the candelabrum above their heads and set her cheeks on fire.

"Oh, how dare you?" she said, her bosom heaving. "How dare you!"

His lips drew up at the corners.

"That is better," he said. "Now you have some color about you. You need not answer my question, by the way. It was purely rhetorical. And purely cosmetic."

She felt a horrifying urge to laugh. He had done it again — brought color to her cheeks, that is. And it had apparently been deliberate both times. But she was not going to take such treatment meekly.

"Are *you?*" she asked him. "*Virginal,* that is?"

He pursed his lips and gazed at her with half-closed eyes. Equally as horrifying as the urge to laugh a moment ago was the frisson of heated awareness she felt now. She had just asked him in front of half the *ton,* all of which was watching them . . .

"If you are asking whether you may expect fumbling ineptness on our wedding night, Lady Annabelle," he said, "I will simply advise you to wait and see."

The rush of aching awareness

settled unmistakably between her inner thighs.

He was behaving very badly.

So was she, but she had been provoked.

It was a good thing that so many dancers were now on the floor that their nearest neighbors had to shuffle close enough to be within earshot. Their conversation must become more decorous.

"Lady Annabelle," he said, raising his voice slightly — it acquired a bored cadence, "may I compliment you on your appearance tonight? You put to shame the delicate beauty of all the roses and other flowers in the room."

"Thank you, sir." She inclined her head in gracious acknowledgment of the compliment.

And the music began.

If the *ton* had expected him to clump about the ballroom with vulgar ungainliness, they were to be disappointed. He danced gracefully and was light on his feet. He knew all the steps and intricate figures without making one false move. His fingers were warm and sure about Annabelle's when the dance required them to join hands and steady on her waist when he twirled her down the set between the row of ladies on one side and gentlemen on the other.

He had, of course, attended balls before tonight, though most of the *ton* had probably not noticed him. Annabelle had seen him more than once. She had never danced with him, though — until now.

Oh, she could have enjoyed it under

different circumstances. But these were not different circumstances.

He gazed steadily at her throughout the almost half hour of the set. He made no attempt to converse, and he did not once smile.

It was most disconcerting. It was, she guessed, meant to be.

She smiled — dazzlingly — at him the whole while.

He spoke again as the music drew to an end.

"Walk out on the balcony with me," he said. "It is as hot as hell in here."

"Perhaps you do not understand," she said, "that two people do not monopolize each other's company for two sets in a row or for more than two in a whole evening."

"Coal thickening the blood makes one slow of understanding," he said

— in his father's thick north country accent.

Lord Huey and Miss Coolidge were beside them and must have heard the exchange. They would be falling all over their feet to return to the side-lines to repeat it, Annabelle thought.

"Come anyway," Mr. Mason said. "This is my engagement ball, and if that does not entitle me to take my betrothed onto the balcony when I choose, then what use is a be-trothal?"

"An interesting question," she said, "to which I have no definitive answer. Lead the way, sir."

And she laid her hand on his sleeve and half-trotted beside him as he strode in the direction of the French windows without glancing to left or to right.

Was he being deliberately . . . uncouth?

But of course he was!

"They expect it of me," he said as they stepped out onto the balcony, as though he had read her thoughts.

"And you always give people what they expect?" she asked.

"Oh, always," he said with a weary sigh, "when it suits me."

He took her to stand by the rail across from the ballroom and stood with his back to it — in full view of anyone inside who cared to glance their way.

"One would not wish to sully your reputation, after all," he said by way of explanation, "by skulking in the shadows."

"I am overwhelmed by your consideration for my reputation," she told him.

He looked at her and pursed his lips.

"This has all been very hard on you, has it not?" he said.

She smiled and fanned her cheeks.

"But not at all on you," she said.

It was not a question.

He raised his eyebrows.

Despite her white gown, she looked breathtakingly lovely. There were silver threads in the fine fabric, and they shimmered in the candlelight. The garment, what little there was of it, had probably cost a king's ransom. It was cut low at the bosom, which was lifted enticingly by her stays, and clung in soft folds to her slender, shapely form. It left little to the imagination, but in her case reality surpassed even the most salacious of imaginations. She was not particularly tall, but her legs, outlined beneath the flimsy fabric, were long and slim.

Her very blond hair was piled high in intricate curls, with wavy tendrils left to trail artfully along her neck and over her temples. Her eyebrows arched over thick-lashed blue eyes. A straight little nose drew attention downward to a mouth that was graced with soft, very kissable lips.

She was a rare beauty.

It was a pity she had eloped with a coachman. She might have married a prince. Or Illingsworth, who would be a duke one day and had been besotted with her until she disgraced herself. And very rich, of course.

It was a pity she was now doomed

to marry a coal merchant's son.

Reggie, well aware that he was on public display even if they *were* outside the ballroom, looked her over coolly — even insolently — while he stood with his back to the balcony rail and she stood a few feet distant, half turned toward him, half toward the ballroom as if she would flee for safety at any moment if he gave her mortal offence.

She had just given *him* mortal offense. Did she believe all this business had caused her more suffering than it had him? That she had some sort of exclusive ownership of the suffering business?

Guests strolled by arm-in-arm inside the ballroom, waiting for the next set to begin. A few couples came out onto the balcony and strolled farther along. All, without being at all obvious about it, were observing the two of them, hoping for . . . what?

"What, do you suppose," he asked, "are they all expecting?"

"Of us?" She turned her head to look fully at him. All evening, even when she had been smiling, she had looked cool and aristocratic. The ice maiden. Except, of course, when he had provoked a blush in her pale cheeks and a flash of indignation in her eyes with his question about virginity. He enjoyed discomposing her. "A cool civility, I suppose."

"And is that what we are going to give them?" he asked her. "How tedious!"

"You would prefer," she said, "that I walk away and ignore you for the rest of the evening?"

"That would be even more tedious," he said.

She raised the fan that was dangling from her wrist, opened it, and wafted it before her face despite the fact that it was rather cool out on the balcony.

"You do not intend, surely, to keep me at your side all evening?" she asked. "People might begin to think that we *welcome* this situation in which we find ourselves."

"On the other hand," he said, "they might think me blind and daft if I do not show *some* sign of appreciation for the beauty my father's fortune has bought me. You made a bold move choosing that particular gown to wear this evening, even if it *is* a virginal white. It is also rather . . . provocative, is it not?"

Her fan closed with a snap.

"You would have me dress in a black shroud, then?" she asked him. "Or in sackcloth and ashes?"

"It might be itchy," he said. "The sackcloth, I mean. And ashes might make me cough when I dance with you. And black? No, I think not. You will note that I have not complained of your choice of attire. I would have to have nothing but tar running in my veins not to appreciate it."

"You are being deliberately . . ." She made circles in the air with her fan, but could not seem to draw from the air the word she wanted.

"Vulgar?" he suggested. "Uncouth?"

"Annoying," she said. One white-slippered foot was tapping a tattoo on the wooden floor of the balcony. She opened her fan with a flourish

again. "As though all this were a *joke*."

He shrugged.

"I always have preferred comedy to tragedy," he said.

The orchestra began playing, and the dancers within bowed and curtsied and pranced into vigorous action. It was one of those country dances that tested one's endurance. A number of nondancers stood, as though by chance, close to the French windows, one eye and one ear turned to the balcony. If they could have stretched out their closer ear as they could an arm, they would surely have done so.

"Step closer," Reggie said.

"What?" She looked startled, and her fan stilled again.

He reached out one hand toward

her and, after regarding it suspiciously for a few moments, she set her free hand in it. He closed his fingers about hers. Through her glove her hand was warm and slender.

"Step closer," he said again.

"Why?" She looked at him with considerable wariness, but she took three-quarters of a step in his direction.

He inhaled the subtle scent of lilies-of-the-valley.

"I believe," he said, "the *ton* would be thrilled — *scandalized* and thrilled — if I were to steal a kiss from you."

The light was behind her. He could not swear that her cheeks were aflame, but he guessed they were. Certainly her eyes widened.

"You would not dare!" she exclaimed.

"Would I not?"

He regarded her lazily and guessed that a sizable number of the ball guests were already fully aware that they were on the balcony together, he and Lady Annabelle Ashton, and that they were holding hands and standing rather indecorously close to each other. How very foolish high society was. It was quite willing to condone almost any vice, provided it was performed discreetly and privately. It was titillated and outraged by any mark of apparent affection between two people who were affianced.

Especially two who had been forced together under scandalous circumstances.

"It would be unpardonably vulgar," Lady Annabelle said.

"Which is what the highest sticklers expect of me," he said. "It is even what they *want* of me so that they may go on their way tonight satisfied that they have not wasted an evening of the Season on the usual bland entertainment."

"We should go inside now," she said. "I am chilly."

"Liar," he said. Her hand had turned hot in his, though whether with embarrassment at the thought of being kissed or desire that it happen was not clear. "And a kiss would have another positive result. It would restore some sympathy for you, especially if you were to return to the ballroom immediately afterward, smiling bravely but in obvious distress. You would be seen to be suffering dreadful consequences for your great indiscretion."

"You are *enjoying* all this, are you not?" she said from between her teeth.

He thought about it. Actually he was.

"And you are not enjoying *your-self?*" He gazed deeply into her eyes, shadowed as they were by the darkness of the night.

"Papa has made it very clear to me," she said, "that if I am ever to be fully forgiven by the *ton,* there must not be even a *hint* of scandal in my behavior for the rest of my life."

"I will not stand for such a boring wife," he said. "You will have to choose between Papa and me."

"No," she frowned. "I will never do that. I have never been willing to do that."

He raised his eyebrows.

"But you will owe me obedience after we are married," he reminded her — just to be provocative.

He was not disappointed.

"If you ever try to hold me to that ridiculous marriage vow," she said, bristling visibly and raising her voice, "I will fight you to the death with every weapon in my arsenal. And don't think I do not possess a few."

Someone — Reggie did not turn his head to see who — had stopped strolling a short distance away on the balcony and was giving them unabashed attention.

The unhappily betrothed pair were already quarreling.

Reggie grinned.

"That sounds promising," he said, waggling his eyebrows and keeping a wary eye on her fan.

"I *mean* it."

She obviously did. Her nostrils flared. Her eyes glared. Her one hand was rigid in his own. The other tightened predictably about her fan.

"I sincerely hope you do," he said soothingly. "You can fight me any day you want, Lady Annabelle Ashton — or any night for that matter. *Especially* any night."

Indignation did marvels for the bosom of a lady wearing stays and a flimsy gown. Hers heaved and looked for a moment as if it might pop free of her bodice. Alas, it did not happen. But it drew Reggie's eyes, and it heated his blood.

"This is not kind of you," she said, lowering her voice again.

Kind?

He searched her eyes, but they were huge pools of shadow and darkness.

"Is it not?" he murmured.

"No." There was a slight tremor in her voice.

He pulled slightly on her hand and lowered his head and set his lips to hers. They were soft and warm and slightly moist. He set the tip of his tongue to the seam at the center of her lips and pressed it hard and deep into her mouth.

She made a low and startled sound in her throat.

He withdrew his tongue and his lips and released her hand. He leaned back against the rails again and smiled at her with half-closed eyes.

"Very nice," he said and wondered where all the air had gone in their vicinity.

He must *not* get an erection. That would be going too, too far into vulgarity. He had to use all his will-power to avoid one, though. For the merest moment she had sucked on his tongue.

She was staring at him, with parted lips and hands balled into fists at her sides. She would be fortunate if her fan did not snap in two.

"You had better run along," he said, "looking like a brave, smiling martyr. On second thought you had better not run. A lady never runs, does she? I shall claim a waltz with you later in the evening."

She turned without a word and walked back into the ballroom, her steps unhurried, her posture perfect. He would wager half a fortune she was smiling and looking coolly about her, avoiding eye contact with no one.

Always and ever she had pluck.

And she was making her way, he could see, toward his mother.

He had behaved as he would have been expected to behave. He had been almost but not quite vulgar. He had been forced into this marriage by his own extravagance, but he was not above taking advantage of the fact that his betrothed was beautiful and desirable.

That was how everyone would see it.

His mother would be pleased, though perhaps a little anxious lest he dishonor Lady Annabelle more than she had already dishonored herself. His father would be ecstatic. *Her* mother would be cautiously optimistic. Her father . . .

Well, there was no pleasing Havercroft. It was best not to waste time trying. Not that he always did what was best.

Lady Annabelle had set both her hands in his mother's, and Ma was beaming happily and affectionately at her. He could not see his betrothed's expression.

On the whole, Reggie thought, this ball was probably a success. The *ton* would engage in happy speculation about whether they hated each other or felt some attraction to each other. Their parents would see that they were circling warily about each other, partly hostile, partly civil, partly willing to settle for some amicable sort of arrangement since their marriage to each other was not to be avoided.

He pushed himself away from the

rail and strolled back into the ballroom. This current set would be ending soon and he was going to have to make himself agreeable with some other partners before he claimed his betrothed again for the waltz.

He stared down several male smirks from those gentlemen who rarely danced but always parked their persons in the best place from which to observe scandalous goings-on upon which to report in numerous fashionable drawing rooms the following day.

His eyes settled upon Lady Havercroft, who was standing alone and observing the dancing with a smile that appeared to contain equal parts haughtiness and wistfulness. He suspected that the haughtiness was part of a mask she frequently wore. She was not unlike her daughter in that way.

He made his way toward her.

She did not deserve unhappiness. Lady Annabelle was her only daughter — her only child. The events of the past two weeks — not even so long — must be deeply distressing to her.

He must do his best to charm her, to console her, to convince her that her daughter might yet expect some joy out of life — with him.

Yes, he really must.

6

Four Years Ago

On the day after her eighteenth birthday, Annabelle went for a walk alone.
She had to sneak away when no one
was looking, for the house was still
full of aunts and uncles and cousins
who had come to stay for the occasion. Inviting them had been her
papa's way of consoling her for not
being allowed to make her come-out
during the spring Season. But she
would be *eighteen* in August, she had
protested when he had left for London with her mama just before Eas-

ter. And so she would be, he had agreed, chucking her under the chin as though she were still a child, and by this time next year she would be ready to make her curtsy to the queen and enjoy all the entertainments of a Season. But *this* year she would remain at home, and they would celebrate her special birthday by inviting as many family members as were able to come.

And of course her birthday really had been a jolly romp. Several young people from the neighborhood had come for the party yesterday. They had even danced in the drawing room. And Jamie Sewell had found the opportunity to *kiss* her. It had been her first-ever kiss. And she liked Jamie. She had even woven a few romantic dreams about him recently.

But the kiss had been disappointing. His dry lips had pressed so hard against her own that her teeth had bruised the flesh on the inside of her mouth.

So much for romance. And so much for Jamie.

Miriam Sewell, Jamie's sister, had mentioned — in a low, conspiratorial voice to a group of young ladies — that Reginald Mason was at home and that he was more gorgeous than ever. They had all gasped and giggled. Caroline Ashton, Annabelle's cousin, had asked who Reginald Mason was and *was* he coming to the party, but she asked the question at normal volume and was urgently shushed by everyone else in the group. Everyone knew that the name of Mason was not supposed to be uttered at all at

Oakridge Park.

That was all that had been said on the subject apart from a whispered explanation to Caroline and more stifled giggles.

But Annabelle had lain awake thinking about him long after going to bed. Reggie. She had scarcely set eyes on him for four years. They had been friends as children, until she had been caught some distance from the house one day and had been appointed a new, more vigilant young nurse to replace her old nurse, who had gone into retirement in a cozy cottage provided, with a pension, by Papa. And Annabelle and Reggie had been friends again for three summers when they were older. Not that they saw each other frequently during those years. He was not often at home, and sometimes when he was, *she* was away. And since they had never made any definite arrangement to meet, they often missed each other, going to the oak tree by the river on different days. It had not mattered. They were not bosom pals.

It had not mattered to *him*. It had always mattered to her. She had fallen violently in love with him when she was twelve, though she would not have admitted it for worlds — not to anyone at all, even Miriam, her closest friend. And it was all very well for people to laugh at the idea of a twelve-year-old falling in love. It was all very well to speak with amused contempt of *puppy* love. It could still be intense and enduring. She knew. It had happened to her.

She had never fallen out of love

with him, in fact, even though they had not met since the summer she was fourteen and he seventeen. Oh, she had not sighed over him every day of those four years. Sometimes she did not even think of him for days at a time, and she looked forward with some eagerness to having a string of beaux after she made her come-out. But there was always a part of her heart that softened into tenderness when she *did* think of him, or on the rare occasion when she spotted him in the village or at church, which he did not attend much any more.

She walked alone the morning after her birthday because sometimes the fact that Mama and Papa and her aunts and uncles and older cousins treated her as if she were still a child was irksome. And because she had not enjoyed her first kiss and wanted to avoid Jamie if he walked over to the house with Miriam, as he had said he might. She rather feared that he *had* enjoyed the kiss and hoped to pursue some sort of courtship with her, though Papa would have something to say about that, of course. And she walked alone because Reggie was at home and she had not seen him and probably would not do so before he went away again.

She wandered through the trees to the east of the house, trying not to admit to herself that she was heading for the river and the oak tree. She went there quite often, actually. It was a beloved place, soothing to her soul. It was also the place where she could indulge rather melancholy dreams.

She walked to the oak tree when it came into sight and set her hand against the ancient trunk. She liked the idea that the tree had probably stood in the same place for perhaps a few hundred years, living and enduring. She set her forehead against the bark and inhaled.

It was not a perfect day. Although the air was warm enough, there were clouds overhead, and the wind was brisk enough to ruffle the surface of the river.

She wandered to the bank and kneeled down to gaze into the water. She could not see any fish today. Perhaps they had found some cozy spot in which to shelter until the water was calmer. She trailed the fingers of one hand in the water. It was not cold.

She remembered a skinny little boy, his drawers almost falling off his nonexistent hips, crashing into the water as he leapt from the tree. She smiled at the memory.

"A penny for them," a deep male voice said.

She looked up, startled. He was standing at the other side of the river, looking breathtakingly splendid in a form-fitting coat and tight pantaloons and shining Hessian boots. He looked far more suited to tea in the drawing room than a tramp in the outdoors. His hair, thick and dark, was fashionably disheveled. Though perhaps that was accidental. The wind was blowing it about his head. He wore no hat. His features were chiseled and handsome. He was a man now. He must be twenty-one years old.

"You have given up trespassing in your old age?" she said, smiling at him.

"Maybe I will when that time comes," he said, "but not a day sooner. Shall I come over there?"

"How?" she asked.

"There is a bridge higher up," he said, pointing to his right.

"There is?" She knew of no bridge.

"Come and see."

He grinned at her and turned to walk along the bank on his side. She kept pace with him on her side.

"It was my eighteenth birthday yesterday," she said, lest he think she was still a child.

"Yes, I know," he said. "Did you enjoy your party?"

Ah, he knew about that, did he? He

must be the only young neighbor who had not been invited.

"I did," she said.

"And did you have lots of gifts?" he asked.

"I did," she said again. "I had a diamond on a silver chain from Mama and Papa. I will wear it at my come-out ball next spring."

"And be the belle of the ball," he said. "But you would be even without the diamond. You have grown into a lovely woman."

There! Another gift, the most precious of all.

"Thank you, Reggie," she said. "You have not turned out so badly yourself."

She laughed lightly, and he joined in.

"There it is," he said, pointing

ahead, and she could see that it was not a bridge to which he had referred but rather a collection of large, flattish stones embedded in the river bottom and poking above the surface of the water. They were stepping stones of a sort, she thought, though they looked alarmingly far apart.

"You will fall in," she said.

"Watch me."

And of course he did not. He hopped from one stone to the other with sure footing and no hesitation at all. Within moments he was on her side of the river, looking down at her and grinning. He was maybe three-quarters of a head taller than she instead of what had seemed like three feet taller when she last saw him. And suddenly he seemed very close.

"Hello, Anna," he said, as if they

were just meeting.

"Hello, Reggie."

Her heart was pounding and there was a funny look in his eyes, and she had to stop herself from blushing and giving away her secret. How very humiliating *that* would be.

"Have you had *your* birthday yet?" she asked him, turning away to stroll back in the direction of the oak tree.

"I have," he said. "In May. I am of age. My father did not give me a diamond, though. He gave me a house and park."

"What?" She turned her head to look at him.

"In Hampshire," he said. "But with strings attached. It will be legally mine when I turn thirty or when I marry, whichever comes first. In the meantime, my father retains ownership. But it is mine for all intents and purposes."

"Your own *home,*" she said. "Are you going to live there?"

"I already do," he said. "I have come here for a few days to sort through some of my things."

They were back at the oak tree. She stopped walking and leaned back against it.

"Oh, Reggie," she said, "you are all grown up."

"And you," he said. "Just look at you."

He stood a couple of feet from her and did just that, letting his eyes roam over her from head to toe.

"You grew after all," he said, and he smiled his slightly lopsided smile — it was gorgeously attractive — and she knew he did not just mean that she had grown upward. She had been a late developer. Even at fourteen she had still looked like a beanpole.

"Eighteen years old," he said, "and never been kissed, I daresay."

"I certainly *have* been kissed," she said, bristling.

He grinned.

"Have you?" he said. "How many times? And by whom? I may have to challenge someone to pistols at dawn."

"By Jamie Sewell," she said triumphantly. "Yesterday, during my party."

"Sewell?" He frowned in thought. "The one with too many teeth and oily hair?"

Jamie *did* have a rather toothy smile, which he flashed about frequently when there were young ladies in the vicinity.

"He does *not* have oily hair," she said, "except when he forgets to wash it."

He chuckled.

"Did you enjoy it?"

"Oh, Reggie," she said. "I did not."

His grin held.

"Why not?"

"His lips were so *dry,*" she said. "And he pressed too hard. My teeth almost cut the inside of my mouth."

She was aware of the sudden rush of color to her cheeks, and she laughed. What *was* it about Reggie that made her relax and treat him like her closest friend at the same time as she ached with unrequited love for him?

"That was a nasty experience for you to have on your eighteenth birthday," he said, his eyes dancing with merriment. "You are likely to remember it all your life unless some other memory obliterates it pretty soon."

"Yes," she said, still smiling. "I will have to remember all the dancing and gifts and fine food."

"Or your second kiss," he said.

"Oh, I —" She was about to protest that she was not going to allow Jamie within ten feet of her for at least the next year or two. But somehow all the air had been sucked away from about the oak tree, and while her breath was suspended, she understood what he meant.

She closed her mouth and swallowed awkwardly.

"If you are offering your services, Reggie," she said, "it is really quite unnecessary. I would hate to have *two* disappointing kisses to remember."

And she laughed again.

"Well, that does it," he said, taking a step forward. "I cannot go away from here with *that* slight on my manhood."

"I did not mean —" She set a hand against his chest as though to hold him away.

"Oh, yes, you did," he said. "I have to prove myself now. *And* give you a happier memory."

And even as her knees threatened to give out beneath her he leaned closer and set his mouth to hers. *Mouth* rather than lips. His lips were parted, and she could feel the warm, moist flesh beyond them. It was a light touch, but it enclosed her own lips, and indeed seemed to enclose *her* in magic and heat and longing.

She felt his tongue touch the center of her lips and rub lightly back and forth across the seam so that a sensation to which she could not put a name stabbed downward through her whole body to come to rest between her inner thighs. And then his tongue was pressing through her lips and past her teeth right into her mouth.

And then both it and his mouth were gone.

Annabelle opened her eyes to find herself gazing into his mere inches away. His eyes looked a mile deep, and she could feel herself falling into them.

"Reggie," she said so softly she was not sure any sound had actually passed her lips.

"Anna." She felt rather than heard the sound of her name.

And then one of his arms slid about her shoulders, the other about her waist, and he drew her away from the tree and against him. She wrapped her own arms about him, and he kissed her again.

Annabelle lost all track of time and place, though afterward she guessed that the kiss lasted no longer than a minute or two.

He was the one who ended it. He tipped his head back from hers, his arms still about her.

"Better?" he said.

She stared at him, uncomprehending.

"Than the first," he explained.

"Oh," she raised her eyebrows. "Yes. Really much better. But I daresay it was Jamie's first as well, you see, whereas I would guess you have had a great deal of practice."

His eyes laughed into hers.

"You will remember it?" he asked.

She considered the question.

"Sometimes," she said. "When I have nothing better to do."

He laughed and released her. He took a step back.

"Will *you?*" she asked. "Remember, that is."

"Oh, always," he said, setting his right hand over his heart. "Forever and a day."

She laughed.

"Reggie," she said, "that was really very naughty of you."

"It was, wasn't it?" he agreed. "I am going to have to be off, Anna. I have a thousand and one things to do before leaving tomorrow."

She felt a little as if her stomach

had dropped into her shoes. She smiled at him.

"And I am going to have to hurry home," she said. "We have a houseful of guests, and I have been truant for long enough. Besides, Miriam Sewell is coming over some time today, and *Jamie* is going to bring her."

He grinned once more, turned away, and strode off back in the direction of the stepping stones without another word or a backward glance.

Annabelle fought tears. There was no point in even trying to fight the empty, bereft feeling within.

That had not really been a kiss, just a demonstration. It had meant nothing whatsoever to him.

And everything in the world to her. She pushed away from the old oak and strode off back in among the trees. It would not do for him to see her standing there looking dazed and forlorn when he got to the other side.

Reggie.

Ah, Reggie.

7

For three weeks Annabelle saw very little of her betrothed, and even when she did, it was always in company with other people. They drove in Hyde Park in an open barouche one afternoon, their mothers seated opposite them. Those two ladies, strangely enough, appeared to get along well with each other. Annabelle was glad about that.

There was a visit to the theater one evening, one to a private concert, another to a ball at which they danced twice together, and there was a dinner at Havercroft House, to which Reginald Mason was invited but not his parents. It was a deliberate snub, Annabelle guessed. The other male guests were all peers of the realm, and the conversation centered almost exclusively about the business of the Upper House, of which they were all members. It seemed to Annabelle that her father deliberately steered it that way. It was a breach of good manners unusual for him, for it precluded the ladies from participating. It also precluded her betrothed, and that, she suspected, was the whole point.

She was made to feel humiliated on his account — and that, surely, was part of the point too.

Her father, who had always indulged her and loved her, had been hurt, and he was not going to forgive her in a hurry.

And now, less than a week before the nuptials, they — Annabelle and her parents — had been invited to take tea with the Masons and a few members of their family who had come to town for the wedding.

Annabelle's father was determined not to go. But Mama put her foot down, something she rarely did, though it was almost always effective when she did.

"Mr. Mason's *money* is good enough for you, William," she was saying sharply on the day the invitation arrived, as Annabelle set her hand on the drawing room door to join them, "and his son is good enough for your daughter, even if only as a punishment. It behooves you, then, to accept a civil invitation to tea when it is offered."

"Mason will boast of it for a decade," Papa complained as Annabelle stayed where she was on the other side of the door for a moment longer.

"And you will grumble about it for twice as long," Mama retorted. "Enough, William! Mr. Mason is just a man, when all is said and done."

"Precisely," he said. "He is a *man,* not a *gentle*man."

Annabelle pushed the door open, and no more was said on the subject except that Mr. and Mrs. Mason had invited them to tea and they were going.

"And no sulking when you are there, miss," her father told her. "You will mind your manners."

Mama merely looked at him, her

eyebrows arched up onto her forehead.

All three of them presented themselves for tea at the Mason house on Portman Square on the appointed afternoon.

Annabelle felt her mother stiffen and her father freeze when the butler threw back the drawing room doors to announce them. The room was large and square — and it was almost bursting at the seams with people. It was also all but pulsing with the sound of loud, hearty conversation and laughter, most of the former conducted in broad north country accents.

And then silence fell, almost as if every conversation in the room had been sliced with a sharp knife, cutting off sentences and leaving even words unfinished.

Every head turned their way.

Mr. and Mrs. Mason hurried toward them, both of them smiling warmly, both with hands outstretched. Reginald Mason was coming more slowly behind them.

"Havercroft!" Mr. Mason boomed, and Annabelle could only guess at how startled her father felt about having his hand grasped by Mr. Mason's two and pumped vigorously up and down. "Grand of you to come. And you too, Lady Havercroft." He repeated the hand pumping with her. "And Lady Annabelle, as lovely as ever."

He folded her into a bear hug and kissed one of her cheeks.

Mrs. Mason, meanwhile, was bobbing curtsies and welcoming her guests to her home with considerably less volume than that employed by her husband. She did hug Annabelle after him, though.

"How nice to see you again, my dear," she said. "You look lovely in pink. It adds color to your cheeks. Come and meet our family. A few of them have come all the way from the north of England for Reginald's wedding. And we invited a few close friends too. I hope you don't mind."

The few family members looked like a vast number to Annabelle. So did the close friends, though she had no way of knowing which were which. The Masons, she concluded, had a different definition of *a few* than her own.

Reginald Mason was bowing politely and murmuring something

largely inaudible.

"Let me introduce you to everyone," Mrs. Mason said, tucking Annabelle's arm beneath her own and patting it reassuringly. "They are all eager to meet you."

Her son was offering Mama his arm.

"Come and meet everyone, Havercroft," Mr. Mason was saying in his booming voice as he rubbed his hands together.

And they proceeded about the room, all of them, Annabelle smiling and inclining her head as everyone was introduced by name and their relationship to everyone else was explained until she felt as if her head must be spinning on her neck. She was making a vain attempt to commit all the details to memory and to remember which face went with which details.

"There is no test at the end of it all," Mrs. Mason said, patting Annabelle's hand as they stood smiling at the last group of six equally smiling people who all resembled one another to a remarkable degree. "You are not expected to remember everyone, my dear."

Everyone obligingly laughed and assured her that indeed she was not.

"But you will know them all eventually," Mrs. Mason said. "You will be married to Reginald, and we are a close family."

Her father, Annabelle saw in a quick glance, was looking his haughtiest and most aristocratic. She could be sure that *he* was making no attempt whatsoever to memorize faces and names or who was second cousin or first cousin twice removed to whom. Her mother, on the other hand, was smiling graciously — even warmly — at everyone.

"You may sit over here if you wish," Mrs. Mason said when everyone had been introduced. She indicated a group of three empty chairs, which had clearly been set up and kept empty for their use. "You may relax and enjoy your tea. Everyone is satisfied now that they have met you. My family and Bernie's have not met a real live earl and countess before. And of course, they were all eager to meet Reginald's bride."

Annabelle's father sat down without further ado.

Her mother, still on Reginald Mason's arm, was talking with the last group to whom they had been introduced. She was being polite.

And so must *she*, Annabelle thought. She had hurt Papa lately. Deeply hurt him and forced him into doing something that would perhaps forever humiliate him. Not that she was responsible for his reckless investments and expenditures, it was true. But she might have released him by marrying the Marquess of Illingsworth. He would have felt far less shame over that solution to his problems than this.

She loved him. She loved both him and Mama. She would make all this up to them if she possibly could.

She smiled at Mrs. Mason.

"If you do not mind, ma'am," she said, "I will talk with some of your other guests and perhaps retain at least *some* of their names for future reference. Mrs. Duffy over there is your sister, is she not? And her daughter is Helen?"

As soon as Mrs. Mason, looking very pleased indeed, confirmed the identification, Annabelle crossed the room to those two ladies and their group and began a conversation with them. She moved from group to group for the next hour, speaking with almost everyone in turn.

She actually rather enjoyed herself. A north country accent might be vulgar by her father's definition, but it was attractive to her ears. She liked the hearty laughter these people did not even try to restrain when something amused them — and much did.

She *liked* them, and she felt that they liked her — or that they were prepared to do so after getting to know her a little better. Surely many of them, if not all, knew the story of her elopement with Thomas Till, but no one shunned her or looked coldly or disdainfully at her.

Her mother was also moving about the room, on Reginald Mason's arm for a while and then alone.

Her betrothed, Annabelle saw with a twinge of unease, had moved from her mother to her father, who had been sitting in haughty isolation, bowed and scraped over by everyone who passed close by him but approached by none except the servant who fetched him tea and cakes.

Reginald Mason first stood addressing her papa and then sat in the seat next to his. He was talking and smiling. Her father appeared to be listening, a curl of distaste to his lips.

Oh, dear, was this wise?

"Lady Annabelle," one fresh-faced, gap-toothed, pretty young girl asked — Annabelle tried in vain to remember her name, "what is your *wedding* dress like? Are you allowed to *say?*"

"I am not," Annabelle said. "But I *can* tell you how I stood on a pedestal for what felt like ten hours while I was being fitted for it, being turned and prodded and poked as though I were a turkey roasting on the fire."

There was a burst of hearty laughter, and she proceeded to embellish the story.

"It doesn't matter what the dress looks like, lass," one of Reginald's maternal cousins said — he was Harold? Horace? Hector? "You would look just grand in a sack."

215

Another burst of laughter.

Papa and Reginald Mason were gone from their chairs. And from the room.

Both of them.

Together?

People had been hurt, Reggie had realized earlier while awaiting the arrival at the house of his betrothed with Havercroft and the countess. Four people in particular. He had known it from the start, of course, but actually seeing it was different from imagining it.

His father was ecstatic over the turn of events. But he was not a heartless man. Far from it. Despite his wrath over Reggie's extravagance and his declaration that if his son was unhappy with his imminent marriage then he deserved to be, actually his son and his wife meant more to him than all his wealth or ambitions combined. Reggie was quite secure in that knowledge. His father would be miserable with regret if it turned out that the marriage he had insisted upon really was an unhappy one.

So would both mothers. They were very different in personality: his mother openly warm and loving, Lady Havercroft more cool and reserved. But he did not doubt that they both deeply loved their children and would suffer greatly if they believed those children to be doomed to unhappiness.

Reggie felt the burden of guilt over having exposed these three people to anxiety. It was time to set their minds at least partially at ease. It was time openly to reconcile himself to the fact that he was going to spend the rest of his natural life with Lady Annabelle Ashton and to make a public effort to show some regard for her. It must not be too lavish, or no one would believe him. But there must be an end to the open hostilities.

It was Havercroft who worried him most, however. The man had been humiliated, first by his unexpected financial losses and the need to recoup them by arranging a judicious marriage for his daughter, and then by the need to marry her to *him,* the son of a man he hated probably above all others.

Reggie did not find him a pleasant man, and if he wanted, he could choose to look on the downfall of such an arrogant, cold man with some glee. But Havercroft, his future wife's *father,* was to be his father-in-law. Reggie guessed that somewhere deep inside the icy exterior there was love for his wife and daughter — a love they returned.

It was going to be more difficult to reconcile Havercroft to the marriage than it would be to reassure the other three. Reggie somehow considered it important to try, though.

His opportunity came during tea, when the countess and her daughter mingled with his family members and his parents' friends rather than sit apart with Havercroft as the untouchable aristocrats. The earl sat in a lone state and in stony dignity. No one else dared approach him, even if anyone had felt so inclined.

Reggie dared.

"Being a member of a large family," he said cheerfully as he stood beside the earl's chair, a cup of tea in one hand, "can be a marvelous thing on special occasions. It is, alas, a little intimidating for outsiders."

Havercroft looked up from his plate. His eyes were steely.

"I do not intimidate easily, Mason," he said.

Reggie continued, undeterred. "But the thing is with my family," he said, "that they will open their arms to include outsiders who are precious to one of their number, and make insiders out of them in no time at all."

"One would hope," the earl said, "you are not suggesting that I walk gladly into Mason arms."

Reggie smiled at the ludicrous image the words created in his mind.

He sat down on the chair beside the earl's.

"Lady Annabelle will be included," he said, "as soon as she is married to me. Oh, even before then. She is being included now. She will be accepted and loved wholeheartedly by a large group of generous people. She will have a warm and affectionate new family to add to her own."

"That," Havercroft said with heavy scorn, "will be of huge benefit to her."

"Unconditional acceptance and affection are always a benefit," Reggie said. "You must not worry that she will be unhappy. I do not believe she will be."

"I wish her joy in her new status in life," Havercroft said.

It was *very* difficult to like the man,

Reggie thought, but he was Lady Annabelle Ashton's father.

"Will you come down to the library for a few minutes?" he asked, getting to his feet again. "It is quieter down there."

The noise in the drawing room was deafening as everyone tried to talk above everyone else, and almost everything that was said was deemed funny enough to draw great bellows and trills of laughter.

It was a typical family reunion.

Lady Annabelle was talking with Uncle Wilfred, who was as deaf as a post but in fine form. He must have just been dipping into his old stock of stories. She was laughing and dabbing a handkerchief to the corners of her eyes.

Havercroft got to his feet without a

word and followed Reggie from the room. The poor man must wish it were possible to make his escape entirely and slip from the house when no one was looking.

Neither of them sat down in the library. Havercroft went to stand before the empty fireplace, a favorite spot with him in any room, it seemed, while Reggie crossed the room to look out the window onto the square beyond.

"It is altogether possible," he said, "that Lady Annabelle *will* be happy as a member of my broader family. They are not gentlefolk, but then neither was the coach man with whom she ran off a little while ago. Yet she preferred him to the Marquess of Illingsworth."

"I suppose," Havercroft said, "you

will be throwing *that* indiscretion in her teeth for the rest of her life, Mason. Only be thankful that you got what you wanted by hovering like a vulture at my door — a titled wife of the aristocracy."

Reggie turned to face him.

"It is, admittedly," he said, "what my *father* has always wanted. He always wanted to make a gentleman of me. He wanted me to consolidate what I acquired through education by marrying into the gentry class or higher. As far as I was concerned, I always hoped that when the time came eventually to think of marriage, I would be free to choose someone for whom I could care for a lifetime, someone who would care equally for me. Regardless of social class."

The earl's lip curled.

"And yet," he said, "you were very ready to snap up Annabelle when she became available rather than lose everything your father has always lavished upon you."

"I grew up in a close, loving family," Reggie said. "Both the inner circle of my parents and the larger circle of their families. I could not accept anything less for myself. This marriage between Lady Annabelle and myself has been arranged by our fathers for reasons of their own, and circumstances have forced us to accept it. But that does not mean we have to live in bitter hostility for the rest of our days. I am determined to work at cultivating an affection for your daughter, and I am not without hope that she will do the like for me. I am pleased by the fact that she has chosen to mingle with my family in the drawing room instead of sitting apart as my mother thought the three of you might wish to do."

Havercroft regarded him with pursed lips and cold eyes. He seemed to have nothing to say, however.

"I am taking the liberty of guessing," Reggie said, "that your daughter is dear to you. She must have hurt you immeasurably when she ran off with your coachman rather than be forced into marriage with Illingsworth. And I believe it must have hurt you to feel obliged to marry her to me. I am here to tell you, sir, that you need feel no more guilt over that. It is done, and we will make the best of it, Lady Annabelle and I. All things that happen in life, my grandmother once told me — *all* things — happen for a purpose. We *will* make the best of this marriage."

Havercroft stared at him.

"The only grandchildren I can ever expect," he said, "will bear the name of *Mason*. They will be *his* grandchildren too."

"Yes," Reggie said.

"And you have the gall to tell me that *all things happen for a purpose?*"

"Yes," Reggie said again.

"I left a perfectly good cup of tea on the table beside my chair upstairs," Havercroft said and strode off in the direction of the library door.

Reggie followed him back upstairs. He had tried. It was all he *could* do at this juncture.

His betrothed was talking with his mother and two of his aunts. She had color in her cheeks this afternoon.

There was animation in her face. And his mother had been right about her pink muslin dress. She looked vividly lovely. He crossed the room toward her, winding his way in and out of groups of relatives and friends.

". . . make a list as soon as I go home," she was saying, "and memorize it so that by my wedding day I will remember all your names."

"But not necessarily the faces that go with them," Aunt Ada said with a deadpan expression.

Lady Annabelle groaned and the others laughed.

Reggie cupped her elbow in one hand, and she looked at him, startled. She had not seen him approach.

"Have you had enough to eat?" he asked.

"She has not had *anything*, Reginald," Aunt Edith told him. "We have been keeping her too busy talking. And I must say, while I can get a word in edgewise, that you are a *very* fortunate young man indeed."

"I know it, Aunt Edith," he said, setting his free hand over his heart. "But right now I am going to escort my good fortune over to the tea tray so that she can eat and not fade quite away before I can even claim her as my wife."

"Go with him, my dear," his mother said, patting her arm. "You can do with more fat on your bones."

Reggie bent his head to hers when they reached the tea tray, which no one was attending, presumably because all the guests had eaten and drunk their fill long ago.

"I have been assuring your father,"

he said, "that I intend to fall violently in love with you and live happily ever after with you."

"Have you indeed?" She looked haughtily at him. "And I suppose he fell on your neck and shed copious tears?"

"Not quite," he admitted. "And you have been making yourself agreeable to Masons and Cleggs and other assorted family members and friends?"

"It is marginally more entertaining than sitting alone in a corner," she said.

"Is peace to be officially declared, then?" he asked. "It is probably time, is it not? Would you like one of these fairy cakes, or do they have too much cream to be eaten delicately? How about one of these currant cakes instead?"

"Both, please," she said and watched him while he placed them on a plate for her. "Peace does not necessarily mean total amity, only an end to the worst of hostilities. Yes, it may be declared. Cautiously. Everyone would be understandably skeptical if we were suddenly to fall passionately in love."

"Our mothers are happier than they were," he said.

"And your father," she said. "But was he ever *not* happy?"

"Before he heard of your plight and realized how he might use it to his advantage he was a mite annoyed with me," he said. "I had a dashed lot of ill fortune at the tables and at the races, you know."

"Yes," she said. "And you had to fill that room with boots and coats and other faradiddle."

"My valet would not enjoy hearing my lovingly starched neckcloths lumped in with a whole host of other belongings as *faradiddle*," he said.

And then his eyes met hers, and he saw laughter in their depths. At the same moment she bit into the fairy cake and cream shot out of the sides, as he had known it would. He watched, fascinated, as she licked it off the corners of her mouth, leaning forward over her plate as she did so.

Reggie felt an alarming rise in the already-warm temperature of the room, and a corresponding tightening in the area of his groin.

To distract himself from lascivious thoughts, he looked down at her hand, which still held the fairy cake. He took it from her and set it on the plate, careful to hold it where there was only cake. And then, with totally brainless lack of forethought or memory of exactly where they were, he lifted her hand to his lips and licked the cream from the edge of her forefinger and sucked it off her thumb.

He felt like a raging furnace.

And cream had never tasted so delicious.

"Oh." She sounded breathless. And as if she were strangling.

Reggie looked up into her face, and beyond her to a grinning cousin.

He grinned back and took a napkin from the tray to dry her hand and wipe off the remains of the cream.

"A stolen kiss on the balcony at our betrothal ball," he said. "A little finger-sucking at your family tea.

People might well conclude that I am a red-blooded male, Lady Annabelle."

"When in reality," she said, "all you are is a man who does not know how to behave."

"Do I take it," he asked her, "that you do not want to finish your cake? I did warn you. Indeed, I do believe our cook ought to be severely reprimanded for serving such unmanageable delights when we have company."

"Everyone has been remarking upon how delicious they are," she said, taking up her plate again and biting into the remains of the cake.

The cream oozed again, and again she licked it off her lips — looking steadily and defiantly into his eyes as she did so.

Minx!

"The weather has been a bit unsettled lately," he said with cheerful politeness. "Will it settle eventually to sunshine or to rain, do you suppose?"

8

One Year Ago

Reggie had not been home for more than three years. Not to his parents' home, anyway. He had seen them several times in the meanwhile, though. They sometimes came to London when he was there, usually during the spring, when he enjoyed socializing with the friends he had made at school and university and with the sons and daughters of his parents' friends, whom he had known all his life. And they often came to stay with him at Willows End, the home and estate that had been unofficially his since his twenty-first birthday.

He liked being there. He loved the house, an old early-Georgian manor, and the park. And he liked pitching in with the work of the farm, getting his hands dirty with soil, acquiring an all-over sweat, pulling calves from distressed cows, shearing sheep. The farm was even turning a modest profit under his management.

But he was back at home in Wiltshire at last. His mother had been rather poorly last winter. Although she was feeling much better by the time spring came, Reggie's father had felt it unwise to take her to London during the spring or to Willows End during the summer. And so Reggie had come to see *them* in the early autumn, after the harvest was done.

It was one of those weeks in October when one would have sworn it was still summer except that there was a different feel to the air and a different look to the sunlight, and the leaves on the trees were beginning to turn yellow.

It was the middle of the afternoon on the third day of his visit, and he was strolling alone and aimlessly about the park, no particular destination in mind as he feasted his eyes on the landscape surrounding him and enjoyed the warmth. He ought to have come before now despite the fact that he had seen plenty of his parents in other places. This was where he had belonged all his life. It was where his roots were.

Why had he always made excuses

to himself *not* to come? He knew the reason, but his mind skirted about it as it always did. Besides, it was a stupid reason. One simply did not fall in love during the course of a single afternoon when one was twenty-one. In *lust,* yes, certainly. But not in *love.*

It had merely been the attraction of the forbidden.

His aimless steps had brought him, he could see, to that narrow stretch of the river he had always called the bridge. Or *had* his direction been aimless? Had he been making his way here all along? He ought not to cross over to the other side. It would be very embarrassing at his age to be caught and escorted off Oakridge land or, worse, hauled up before a magistrate for trespassing.

He crossed anyway and strolled in

the direction of the old oak tree. It was strange that they had always met there. Their meetings had not been numerous, though they had spanned many years. He would guess that the total number of times could almost be tallied on the fingers of his two hands with a few toes thrown in. But it had always been here. He had been eight the first time, twenty-one the last.

And now again when he was twenty-four.

He could scarcely believe the evidence of his own eyes. There she was, sitting on the grass beside the river, her knees drawn up to support an open book, her neck and face and the pages shaded by a straw-colored parasol.

He could not even be sure that it

was she since the parasol half hid her. But he knew it was. Who else could it be? Besides, there was something within him that *felt* it was she.

She had not heard him. Neither had she seen him. He had approached the river from the opposite direction than usual, and there were not enough autumn leaves on the ground yet to crunch beneath his feet.

He considered turning around and going back the way he had come. There was little to be gained from hailing her. He had seen her occasionally in London during the past three spring Seasons. She had made a hugely successful come-out, being both the daughter of the Earl of Havercroft and at least twice as beautiful as her nearest rival. She could have been married a dozen or more times during those years without moving out of the titled ranks. The fact that she had not married any of her many suitors was an indication that she knew she could be discriminating, that she knew she could wait until she met someone with whom she really wanted to spend the rest of her life.

In three years the gulf between her and Reggie had widened immeasurably — though it had always been impossibly wide.

He had never tried to come face to face with her. Or to speak with her. Or to attract her attention. Occasionally she had seen him. Their eyes had met, held for a few uncomfortable moments, and then broken contact. Sometimes it was she who looked away first, sometimes he.

He took a few steps forward rather than back and rested one shoulder against the tree.

She turned a page.

"Is it a good book?" he asked.

The parasol fell to the grass behind her. Her head turned sharply in his direction, and she stared at him with wide eyes, her eyebrows arched above them in surprise.

Several seconds went by.

"It is a very silly book, actually," she said. "Samuel Richardson's *Pamela*. Papa said I was never to read it because there are passages in it that are not suitable for a lady's eyes. So of course I had to sneak it out of the library and read it for myself. But it is tedious and extremely silly. Mr. B — deserves to be hanged from the nearest tree by his thumbs, but I have the horrible suspicion that Pamela is going to be stupid enough to marry him."

"She is," he said. "They are going to live happily ever after, as rakes and virtuous females invariably do when they marry."

"Poppycock!" she said.

"You have not a romantic bone in your body," he said, folding his arms across his chest. "I can remember the time when you flatly refused to be a damsel in distress and allow me to rescue you and gallop off with you on my trusty steed."

"Was I really such a sensible child?" she asked.

The saucy preliminaries over with, they stared at each other again.

"Anna," he said at last because he really could not think of anything else to say.

"Reggie."

She closed her book then and set it down on the grass beside her before getting to her feet and coming toward him. She was wearing a pale blue dress and spencer and a pretty little straw bonnet.

"I had not heard you were at home," she said, gazing at his face as if to memorize his features. "I saw you at the Wellings's ball in the spring. You danced with Miss Stockwood."

"You must be twenty-one," he said. "You are dangerously close to being on the shelf, are you not?"

"Perhaps no one will have me," she said.

"Or perhaps," he said, "you will have no one. Are you waiting for someone special?"

"Yes," she smiled ruefully. "It is hard to find such a man. Have you started a search for a wife yet, Reggie? Are you finding it equally difficult?"

"You have never found anyone you can love?" he asked her.

"N — ," she started to shake her head, and then gazed deeper into his eyes and sighed. "Yes. Once."

He felt, ridiculously, as though she had just stabbed him with a knife.

"It did not work out?" he asked her. She shook her head.

"He did not love you in return?"

"Oh, no," she said, smiling. "No, he did not. He was young and carefree and wanted nothing more from me than a stolen kiss. Men are very different from women. And that is my profound observation for *this* year."

"Did he *steal* a kiss?" he asked, frowning.

"To be honest," she said, "I did not put up any fight."

"You *wanted* him to kiss you?" he asked her. "And you *enjoyed* it? You *loved* him?"

"This old friend of yours can be very foolish, Reggie," she said, and he felt a deep and quite ridiculous depression.

"Well," he said in sheer self-defense, allowing a slightly mocking smile to lift one corner of his mouth, "this is a blow to my pride, Anna. I thought your *second* kiss, the one given the day after your eighteenth birthday, was the one you would remember for the rest of your life."

He had the sensation suddenly that he was falling into her eyes, and he became aware just as suddenly that they were welling with unshed tears.

"Oh, Reggie," she said so softly that he scarcely heard her.

Well.

Oh, dash it all!

"To which kiss are you referring?" he asked her.

"I have only been kissed twice," she said. "I have never allowed any man to kiss more than the back of my hand since that second time. Foolish, is it not?"

He had always found it characteristic of her to speak frankly of things the average male would not reveal even under torture. She was talking of *him?* She had once loved *him?*

She laughed softly and blinked away her tears.

"Oh, you need not look so frightened, silly," she said. "You only *kissed* me, Reggie. You did not compromise me. I am not going to demand that you do the decent thing and *marry* me. Come, tell me we are still friends even if we scarcely see each other any longer."

And she held out her right hand to him.

"You *loved* me?" he asked her, ignoring her hand.

"I was a mere *girl*," she said, laughing. "Of course I loved you. You were handsome and dashing and *everyone* was in love with you."

"It is past tense, then," he said as she returned her hand to her side. "Not present tense?"

"Oh, Reggie," she said, laughing again. "How silly you are!"

Which did not really answer his

question, did it?

"Tell me about your home," she said. "The one your father gave you for your twenty-first birthday. Do you live there at all? Do you like it? Is it attractive? Oh, I know almost nothing about your life as it is now. Do tell me."

She was smiling brightly — with eyes that were strangely empty. Or guarded. He did not know quite what was wrong with her eyes, but something was.

"Anna," he said, "do you know why I hurried away that day after kissing you?"

Her smile faded and he could read her eyes at last. They were bleak.

"Of course I do," she said. "You had proved your point and were afraid that I would misunderstand and start to talk about *feelings.* Men are such cowards about feelings. But you need not have worried. I knew you felt no tender emotions for me. I did not expect them of you."

"I went away," he said, "because the situation was hopeless. Utterly. I was the son of a man who made his fortune as a coal merchant and made no secret of his roots despite his ambition to move up the social ladder. You were the daughter of an earl who was very conscious of his superiority over other, ordinary mortals. And in addition to that matter of class, there was the additional fact that our fathers had rubbed each other the wrong way for almost thirty years, that they hated each other with a passion. And I do not even know why I use the past tense. The present tense would do just as well. If one wishes to be theatrical — even Shakespearian — about our situation, one would have to say we were star-crossed lovers. Or would have been if . . ." His voice trailed away without completing the thought.

Her eyes were huge again.

"We were not lovers," she said.

"Did you fall in love with me on that day?" he asked her.

"Oh," she looked away suddenly as though something very interesting was happening in the river. "No. I fell in love with you when I was twelve and you were fifteen. You had grown at least a foot since I last saw you, and you had become slender rather than skinny, and your face had turned from boyhood toward manhood and every other girl for miles around agreed that you were gorgeous. We *all* fell in love with you that year, Reggie. But I was the lucky one. You were my friend."

"Ah," he said. "I was a slowtop, then. I fell in love with you when I kissed you, Anna. Or perhaps it would be more accurate to say that it was then that I realized I loved you. And almost simultaneously I realized how impossible it all was. I have never been one to invite unnecessary pain into my life. I left as fast as my feet would carry me on the assumption that I was doing it soon enough to leave all pain behind me."

"And *did* you?" Her voice was abnormally high-pitched.

He shook his head and pursed his lips.

"Memory can be the most damnable thing at times," he said.

"You could not forget?" she asked.

He shook his head again.

She took a step forward and set her forehead against his chest. He lowered his face to her head, encountered the straw of her bonnet, and fumbled beneath her chin until he had pulled loose the ribbons and tossed the bonnet to the ground behind her. He drew the pins from her hair, twined his fingers in it as it cascaded down over her shoulders, and rested his forehead against the top of her head.

She wrapped her arms about his waist and said no more for some time.

He had loved her without ceasing for three years. She had loved him for nine. And the chance for a happy outcome to their love was the same now as it had ever been. Nil, in other words. None whatsoever. Non-existent.

When she tipped back her face to gaze into his eyes, he lowered his mouth to hers.

Before passion and desire took hold of him, body and mind, he marveled at the feeling of homecoming, of rightness. He was where he belonged. So was she. *They* were where they belonged.

Together. In each other's arms.

At last.

He loved her. *He loved her.* The thought pulsed through Annabelle's brain like lifeblood.

She pressed her mouth to his, touched his tongue with her own, tightened her arms about him.

He was *here.* He was *here now,* in the circle of her arms.

But thoughts of wonder and joy were soon replaced with a desire so intense that all else was swallowed up in it.

"Anna."

He was kissing her face, her neck, her throat. His hands were moving over her breasts, down over her waist to her hips and then behind her to cup her buttocks and lift her against him. She pressed her palms hard over his muscled chest and across his broad shoulders. She reveled in the unfamiliar contours of his man's body. She could feel his desire, his need for her pressed hard to her abdomen.

"Reggie."

She sought his mouth with her own again, and all became raw, pulsing need.

But then he was gasping against her mouth and stiffening defensively.

"I must not," he said. "I cannot. It is impossible."

"No," she moaned as she twined her arms about his neck. "It is *not* impossible. Nothing is. Reggie, don't stop. Don't let me go. Please don't stop."

Her mind was not working properly, of course. What she was begging for was shocking under any circumstances. But he was right. It *was* impossible. She could not let him go, though, when he was here at last and his arms were about her and hers about him and nothing else in the world mattered except the two of them.

She preferred not to explore the confusion of her own thoughts. She preferred not to think at all. Not now. Not yet.

"Reggie," she whispered against his mouth, "I love you. I love you."

Perhaps his mind was not working properly either, though he *had* made a valiant effort to be rational. He stopped her whisperings with his mouth, urgent now and abandoned to passion.

And then somehow they were on the grass together, just out of range of the tree roots, ravaging each other's mouth while their hands roamed and explored with fevered intensity. He pulled up her skirts, and she could feel him fumbling with the buttons at the waist of his pantaloons.

And then, as he moved over her, he looked into her eyes, and they both paused. Not to stop entirely. They were too deep into passion for that. But to still the worst of the frenzy, to know what it was they were about to do, to know each other.

She smiled at him, and he smiled back, a moment of peace at the heart of the storm. His dark eyes had depths she had never seen in them before. His hair was ruffled.

"Anna, my love," he said.

She lifted her hand and cupped it about one of his cheeks.

"Reggie," she murmured back to him.

And he came over her, his legs coming between hers and pressing them wide, his hands pushing her skirts up to her waist and then sliding beneath her to lift and tilt her. She bent her legs to set her feet flat against the ground. And she could feel him hard and unfamiliar against her.

She shut her eyes tightly at the shock of his invasion. He was hard, and he was pressing into her, stretching her wide. And then there was the near-panic of knowing there was no more room and the searing pain as he found more. And the final knowledge that she was filled.

She opened her eyes. He had raised himself onto his elbows and was gazing down at her.

"I am sorry," he whispered. "I am so sorry."

He was apologizing for the pain. But it was pain that was also pleasure. And desire.

"Don't be," she was whispering too.

"Oh, don't be."

He kissed her mouth and her jaw, and he drew almost out of her and pressed back in and so set up a slow and steady rhythm. Annabelle closed her eyes again. It was still painful. She was dreadfully sore. It was also the most exquisitely wonderful feeling in the world.

They were making love. He was inside her body. *Reggie* was. She closed inner muscles about him.

She could smell his cologne, feel his heat, hear the wetness of their coupling. And finally, as his rhythm quickened and deepened, pain became indistinguishable from a pleasure that washed over her and engulfed her.

And then he pressed deep and held there, tense against her until she felt a gush of heat deep inside. She sighed with contentment as her toes curled up inside her shoes.

It was done.

And she was not sorry.

Her love was not unrequited, and it was not unfulfilled.

She was entirely happy. The future did not touch her. *Now* was all that mattered.

He lay heavily on her for several moments before lifting his head and gazing into her eyes and kissing her with warm, drowsy lips. Then he sighed, drew free of her body, and rolled off her to lie beside her. With one hand he lowered her skirts, and then he set his own clothing to rights and sat up. He draped his arms over his knees.

Annabelle gazed at him for a while.

She loved him, and he loved her. They belonged to each other. There was no lovelier feeling in the world. She spread one hand across his back.

He sighed again.

"Oh, Anna," he said, "I am *so* sorry. And how inadequate an apology *that* is."

Her hand slid to the ground.

"Because it is all so impossible?" she asked. She was not ready to consider the possibility of the impossible.

He raked the fingers of one hand through his hair.

"We cannot marry," he said. "You know that."

"Would you marry me if you could?" she asked.

He turned his head to look over his shoulder at her, and she held her breath.

"In a heartbeat," he said.

She let go of her breath and smiled.

"We are both of age," she said. "No one can stop us marrying."

He continued to look at her.

"How would your father react," he said, "if you were to announce that you were going to marry me no matter what?"

She stared back at him, and he turned his head away again and stared off across the river.

"Precisely," he said, just as if she had answered him in words. "He would never speak to you again. He would not allow your *mother* to speak to you or anyone else in your family. He would force the beau monde to shun you. You would not be able to bear it."

"I would," she began. But her protest trailed away. She might be able to cope with social ostracism. But estrangement from her mother and father? She closed her eyes. "How would *your* father react?"

"He has always insisted that he hates your father," he said, "and that he does not care a tupenny toss — *his* words — for his good opinion. But he does care. He would be humiliated if I did something to cause your father to despise him even more than he already does."

She lay still and he sat still for what seemed a long while in silence. There seemed to be nothing else to say. They could not marry. But how could they *not?* Especially now.

"Papa wants me to marry someone wealthy," she said at last. "*You* are wealthy."

It was grasping at straws.

He turned his head away so that she could not see even his profile. "The money is black with coal," he said bitterly. "It would soil his hands."

"He has been having expensive renovations done on the house this year," she said. "And he has been losing money he invested a few years ago. A fortune, in fact."

She felt guilty for divulging information that was supposed to be their own ghastly secret. But people would soon find out. They always did.

He said nothing.

"He has been willing to let me enjoy myself for the last few years," she said, "but he is beginning to pressure me to marry the Marquess of Illingsworth, who has fancied himself my suitor since he danced with me at my come-out ball."

"His father is one of the richest men in England," Reggie said.

"Yes."

She heard him inhaling and exhaling slowly.

"The pressure will really be on next spring during the Season," she said.

He got to his feet abruptly and went to stand on the bank of the river.

"Havercroft would never accept my suit, Anna," he said, "even if he knows that my father is as wealthy as the duke. And I daresay he *does* know it. It is pointless to dream."

She lay where she was for a while, gazing upward through leaves that were half green, half yellow to the cloudless blue of the sky beyond. She felt the heavy pull of despair.

"What is left," she asked him, "if there are no dreams?"

But he did not answer.

She got to her feet after a while, brushed her hands over her skirts, and turned to walk away in the direction of home. But she had not walked far before she stopped. The leaves were even more yellow above her head here. It was undeniably autumn. Soon all the leaves would be down and it would be winter. But only a person in the depths of despair neglected to look beyond winter to the spring that inevitably followed, bringing back color and life and hope.

She had left her book and her bonnet and parasol and a whole arsenal of hair pins at the river bank. And something infinitely more precious than any of them. Than anything else in her life, in fact.

She had left her dreams on the river bank.

9

Annabelle was alone with her mother, her maid having settled her flower-trimmed straw bonnet over her elaborate coiffure to her own satisfaction and left the dressing room. It was almost time to leave for church. And it was bound to be full. Almost all of Annabelle's relatives, even those who had not been in town for the Season, had come for the occasion. Large numbers of the Mason family and Mrs. Mason's family, the Cleggs, had come. And almost everyone else who had been invited had returned a card of acceptance.

One could be forgiven, it seemed, for eloping with one's father's coachman, provided one was stopped soon enough. And provided one returned almost immediately to the fold by marrying someone who was almost respectable. And a man as wealthy as Mr. Mason *was* almost respectable, especially when his son, the bridegroom, was quite indistinguishable in speech, education, appearance, and manners from any other gentleman.

People would come out of curiosity, if nothing else. And for the same reason they would keep an eye on the couple for the next year or two, accepting any of their invitations, inviting them to their own entertainments. Eventually Mr. Reginald Mason would be more or less accepted as one of their own, and the scandal surrounding his wife would fade into obscurity.

"I did advise that you wear white," the countess said, "but I am glad you chose the green after all. It is a lovely spring-like color. A *hopeful* color."

Annabelle turned away from the looking glass and hugged her rather tightly, risking creases to both their dresses.

"You have reason to hope, Mama," she said. "I am hopeful myself. I have come to rather like Mr. Mason, and I think he rather likes me. I believe an affection will grow between us."

"And his parents?" her mama asked.

"I adore them," Annabelle smiled warmly.

"Oh," her mother said, sounding

vastly relieved. "And so do I. I always have. I always wished I could speak to them at church and invite them to our parties and go to assemblies they were attending. Now I will be able to do all those things. It would be peculiar if I did not. I believe I can actually make a *friend* of Mrs. Mason."

"Oh, Mama," Annabelle squeezed her hands. "You are not still so dreadfully angry with me, then?"

"Just answer me one question," her mother said. "Did you run away with Thomas Till only so that you would not have to marry the Marquess of Illingsworth? Did you pay him to take you? And did you make sure that you blazed an obvious enough trail so that you would be overtaken very quickly?"

Annabelle squeezed her hands more

tightly.

"You do not need to answer," her mother said hurriedly. "It was all my fault. If I had asserted myself, as I really ought to do far more often than I do, I could have seen to it that your father found someone else for you than the marquess. I cannot think a man in any way attractive when he has bad teeth."

They both snorted with unexpected laughter and ended up with tears in their eyes.

"You *will* be happy with Mr. Mason?" the countess asked. "I have found him surprisingly charming and witty."

But Annabelle had no chance to answer. The door of her dressing room opened again, and her father stood there, looking elegant and austere and unhappy.

"We will be late for church," he said.

He gazed broodingly at his daughter and then said something so very unexpected that both women could only gape at him.

"*If* you want to go, that is, Annabelle," he said. "If you do not, we will take ourselves off to Oakridge before the day is out, and the Masons and the *ton* can go hang for all I care."

It was the most extraordinary declaration of love Annabelle had ever heard from him. The consequences to her father of such behavior would be astronomical in every imaginable way. And catastrophic. And yet he was prepared to do it for *her?*

"Oh, Papa," she said. "I *love* Reginald Mason. Or I will when I know him better, I am sure. I am already falling *in* love with him, and I think he is with me. I really *want* to marry him, reluctant as I was at first. This marriage will *not* be a disaster. You must not feel guilty. None of us must. Oh, *please* let us not feel guilty."

And she closed the short distance between them and flung her arms about his neck.

"But thank you," she said. "*Thank you, Papa. I do love you and Mama.*"

He cleared his throat. He had always been uncomfortable with female emotions, the foolish, dear man.

"We are going to be late," he said, and he stepped back clear of the doorway and offered an arm to each of them.

Annabelle inhaled slowly and deeply. It was her wedding day.

At last.

An hour or so earlier Reggie too had been in his dressing room. It was crowded to capacity with uncles and male cousins. All of them, even the unmarried ones, had advice for the coming years, and particularly for the coming night. Most of the latter was ribaldry they would not have offered if any female ears had been within fifty feet of them.

And then Reggie's mother spoiled it all by coming to see if his cravat and neckcloth were straight. One by one the other men faded away.

"Ma," Reggie said, "if you move my cravat even one millimeter my valet will resign. And I would hate that."

She contented herself with patting him on the chest.

"You would have finished sowing your wild oats soon enough even without all this," she said. "You are a good boy, Reginald. You always have been. A good *man,* I mean. Your father did not have to worry so much. He could afford to pay off your debts."

"Ma." He took one of her hands in his and raised it to his lips. "I am not unhappy. Indeed, I do believe I am actually *happy.* I like Lady Annabelle. I may even be falling in love with her. I am sure I am, in fact. And she seems not entirely indifferent to me."

"Oh," she said with a sigh. "That is exactly what *I* have thought, Reginald. But I fear that perhaps she is a shallow young lady. I *do* hope I am wrong. But how can she be falling in love with you when just a month or so ago she went running off with that coachman?"

"Havercroft was pressing her into a marriage with the Marquess of Illingsworth," he said. "Do you know him, Ma? If you do, you can perhaps understand why she would take such drastic action as making off with the coachman while at the same time making sure that the whole world knew about it."

Her eyes widened.

"It was *staged?*" she said. "She would risk *ruin* rather than marry that marquess, whom I do not know though I am sure I would dislike him intensely if I did."

"My guess is that it was staged," he said. "And if it was, then she was extraordinarily brave and very determined, and I like her the better for it."

"And so do I," she said firmly. "I have *so* wanted to love her without reservation, Reginald, and now I can. And I like her mother too. I do hope the earl will allow us to nod and smile at each other in church, perhaps even to exchange a word or two. And if I were ever to invite her to tea, Reginald, do you suppose she would come?"

"How foolish she would be," he said, kissing her cheek, "if she did not. Ma, don't be unhappy today. Not even a tiny little bit. I fought this betrothal, but now I know it was the best thing that could have happened to me. I am going to do my best to live happily ever after with Lady Annabelle."

She sighed and beamed with contentment, and they both turned to the door as it opened to admit Reggie's father.

"Well, lad," he said, looking his son over from head to toe as he rubbed his hands together. "You look as fine as fivepence. How are you feeling?"

"Nervous," Reggie admitted. "I am terrified that I will drop the ring at the last moment."

"Then you will simply bend down and pick it up," his father said.

They stood and stared at each other, father and son.

"I am sorry, Da," Reggie said, "for all the disappointment I caused you over the winter and spring — as well as all the *money* I cost you. It will not happen again. I promise you."

"This wedding cannot be called off

now," his father said, looking unusually somber. "But I am sorry too, Reginald, for having forced it on you. Sometimes I get blinded by ambition and forget that you and your ma are all that really matter in my life. I would *not* have cut you off without a penny, but it is too late to tell you that now."

Reggie closed the distance between them and held out his right hand.

"Let's forgive each other, shall we?" he said. "And be done with our guilt? And both agree that all has ended well after all? I have just been confessing to Ma that I am quite in love with Lady Annabelle and that I believe she is falling in love with me too. I intend to make a happy marriage of this, Da. And if you are doubtful, then keep watching."

His father did not take his offered hand. Instead, he pulled him into a rough bear hug.

"I will, lad," he said. "I will. And now, if we are not to keep your bride waiting and give the *ton* food for gossip for the next month, we had better be on our way to church. St. George's on Hanover Square, Reginald. Who would have thought I could rise so high in my lifetime as to have a son getting married *there?*"

Reggie offered his arm to his mother. She took it and then linked her free arm through her husband's.

It was his wedding day, Reggie thought, and everyone seemed to be happy about it — at least on his side.

His stomach muscles suddenly contracted uncomfortably. What if he really *did* drop the ring?

10

After the Wedding

By the time the wedding breakfast at Havercroft House had been consumed and most of the wedding guests had taken their leave and the rest had lingered on in the drawing room until evening, the baggage of every Mason relative had been removed from the house on Portman Square and taken to Grillons Hotel. Bags for Reggie's parents had been taken there too. The house had been left empty, apart from servants, for the use of the bride and groom during their wedding night.

The house seemed remarkably quiet, Reggie thought when they arrived there. And strangely unfamiliar, even though it was the same place it had been this morning.

The housekeeper met them very formally in the hall and informed Lady Annabelle that her maid awaited her in the best guest room. She escorted her up there, and Reggie was left to kick his heels and exchange a blank stare with the butler.

He had one drink in the library and took another up with him to his room, where his valet was waiting for him.

Half an hour later, clad in a nightshirt, something he never wore, and a monstrosity of a brocaded blue dressing gown, he tapped on the door of the guest room and opened it when someone murmured something from within.

A branch of candles burned on the dressing table. The bed had been turned down for the night, the drapes pulled back from around it.

His bride was standing over by the window. She wore a white nightgown that was all silk and lace and clung to her perfect curves in a most intriguing fashion. Her very blond hair lay in thick waves down her back.

He closed the door behind his back.

"Anna," he murmured softly.

"Reggie."

"We did it," he said.

"We did," she agreed. "And if you suggest anything remotely like it *ever* again, I will personally clobber you over the head with something very hard."

He struck a thoughtful pose and was silent for a few moments.

"My memory may be defective," he said, "but I do believe it was *you* who suggested when you returned to the river bank that we needed a plan and then rejected the perfectly splendid one I put forward and then dreamed this one up all on your own. I *told* you it was harebrained. I *told* you that once you launched it into motion you would be as helpless as a newborn. And I *told* you I would be bored silly behaving like a spendthrift and a particularly inept gambler. But would you listen to me?"

It was a rhetorical question. He did not expect her to answer it.

"Oh, Reggie," she said. "Your plan

was perfectly *stupid.* Who would have believed that you had dived into the river and hit your head on the bottom and I had dived in to haul you to safety and then took off your wet clothes and warmed you in my arms and held you there until someone finally came along to discover us in such a compromising situation and insist that we marry?"

"Well," he said, "there was no point in suggesting that *you* be the one to hit your head while *I* dived to your rescue, was there? You never would be the damsel in distress, Anna, confess it. And I still think it would have worked splendidly. You would have had to take off your clothes too, though. They would have been wet, remember, when you had dived in after me."

She stared speechlessly at him for a few moments.

"It was *utterly* stupid," she said. "Everyone must know that you swim like a fish while I do not swim at all."

"You don't?" he said, distracted. "So all that business about not getting your hair wet was to save you from having to admit that you would have sunk like a stone if you had dived in?"

"It was no plan at all," she said, avoiding the question.

"And yours *was?*" he said, "even though I had to play the part of a dashed dandy all winter? And then orchestrate matters so that my father reached the end of his tether precisely at the moment when you committed your great indiscretion?"

"*Precisely at the moment?*" she said

her voice rising half an octave. "I languished in my room for *two whole days* before your papa came calling on mine. All I had for company was a *Bible.*"

He grinned.

"Where," she demanded of him, "did you discover that absolutely *mad* Thomas Till?"

"Tillman?" he said. "Did you like him? We were once members of the same drama group at Oxford. His father ran out of funds, and he took to the stage in earnest. He told me after escaping from your elopement that he called himself *Till* 'til he could get back to auditioning for less dangerous roles."

"You have *seen* him?" she said.

"You would not recognize him," he assured her. "Nor would anyone else.

The blond tresses, his most handsome feature, were a wig. He is more than half bald. And he has the gift of all true actors of somehow making himself look completely different with every role he plays even without the use of masks and cosmetics and other tricks. Most of the time he is the most ordinary looking of mortals. He once explained to me that one has to *think* one's way into a part, to *become* the person one is playing. He became your father's dashing coachman and your secret suitor for a while. I hope he was always respectful?"

"I might have known he was an actor," she said. "Whenever we had a few minutes alone together, he spouted bombastic love poetry at me — in *Latin*. At least he *said* it was love poetry. It was probably extracts from Caesar's Gallic wars."

"Probably," he agreed. "You were marvelously brave, love. But I always did say you had pluck, didn't I?"

"It was the first compliment you paid me," she said. "When I was five. I think I fell in love with you at that moment. I am an easy prey to flatterers, you see."

"And to those who sincerely admire you?" he asked her.

"And to them too."

She bit her lip.

"Reggie," she said, "did we do the right thing? It felt perfectly dreadful all the time it was happening — not at all daring and adventurous and exhilarating and *fun.* I had no *idea* I would be so consumed by guilt."

He crossed the room to her in a few

quick strides and caught her up in his arms. And Lord, her nightgown felt virtually nonexistent, and she had been using some wondrously fragrant soap. And she was his bride and this was his wedding night.

She was his *wife.*

The reality of it all swept over him like a tidal wave, as though the rest of the day had been a dream.

"Do the ends ever justify the means?" he said into her hair. "Maybe not. I have felt horribly guilty too, Anna, not least because I consented to let you carry through with a plan in which you had to do the most dangerous parts. But how else *could* we have done it when you were afraid to dive into the river to rescue me from drowning? Short of eloping and alienating our families and society for all time, that is. Our fathers, yours in particular, would never have consented to let us marry if we had simply asked them and used as a reason that we had been friends most of our lives and lovers for one glorious afternoon last autumn."

She wrapped her arms tightly about him and inhaled audibly.

"Oh, Reggie," she said. "You smell wonderful. Do you know what Papa said this morning before we left for church? He said that, if I wished, we need not go, but could run off to Oakridge instead and thumb our noses at the *ton*. He *does* love me."

"I would have looked like a pretty idiot, stranded before the altar at St. George's awaiting a bride who never came," he said. "It would have been the stuff of legends. Were you tempted?"

She tipped back her head and smiled slowly at him.

"I am *almost* tempted to say yes," she said, "just to see the look on your face."

"But you are not going to give in to temptation?" he asked her.

She shook her head.

"I have wanted you since I was twelve years old, Reggie Mason," she said. "Ten long years. Perhaps even longer. I was certainly not going to let you out of my grasp when I had you there."

He rubbed his nose across hers and kissed her softly on the lips.

"Did you say anything to your mother?" he asked her.

"I almost blurted it all out this

morning," she said. "And indeed, I think she may guess part of it. She certainly knows that my elopement with Thomas Till was fake. But you and I agreed that we would not confess the whole of it and risk humiliating any of our parents with the knowledge of how we deceived them. I told her only that I was falling in love with you and that I was almost sure you were falling in love with me."

"I think," he said, "our deceit may have results more positive than just our marriage. I think our mothers will now be able to be friends. I think they have always secretly wanted to be."

She smiled.

"Will we always feel a little bit guilty?" she asked him.

He shook his head.

"Think of the alternative, love," he said.

Her eyes brightened with unshed tears, and she tightened her arms about him.

"They were ten wretched years in many ways," she said. "I despaired of *ever* stopping loving you, even though I tried."

"And now," he said, "you don't have to. And I don't have to pretend to myself that all I feel for you is lust, as I did for three years."

She looked arrested.

"You felt *lust* for me?" she asked him.

"Not at all," he said, grinning and waggling his eyebrows at her. "When I look at you, Anna, I have the same feelings I would have if I were looking at a door."

She laughed, her lovely silvery, amused laughter.

"Are you feeling lust now?" she asked him.

His brow creased in thought.

"I think I might be," he said, and he set one hand behind her and drew her closer until they were pressed to each other in all the strategic places.

"Oh, Reggie," she sighed and melted against him. "I think you are. Oh, I *do* love you."

"Anna." He found her mouth with his and kissed her deeply. "My love. I hope you had plenty of sleep last night. You will not get much tonight. I am going to make love to you over and over until you get as much pleasure from it as I do — and as you did not quite get last autumn. And then, when you *do* share the pleasure, I am going to keep on making love just to prove that it was no freakish accident."

"Words, words, words," she said against his mouth. "When are you going to show me *action,* boaster?"

She laughed softly and then half shrieked as he growled and swung her up into his arms. He strode to the bed with her and tossed her onto it.

"Right, if it is action you want, it is action you will get," he said, divesting himself of the cumbersome dressing gown and nightshirt before joining her there. "My love," he added.

ABOUT THE AUTHOR

Mary Balogh, *New York Times* best-selling author of numerous Regency-era novels, grew up in Wales and moved to Canada to teach. She stayed to marry and raise a family — and fulfill her lifelong dream of being a writer. See her web site at www .marybalogh.com.